Wolf at the Door

Chambray Shifters

Tana Jenkins

Oxford House Publications

Copyright © 2022 by Tana Jenkins

Edited by Alexa Nussio & Brenda Margriet

Cover design by Inkwolf Designs

Originally published by Bryant Street Shorts.

All rights reserved. No part of this publication may be reproduced, stored or transmitted in any form or by any means, electronic, mechanical, photocopying, recording, scanning, or otherwise without written permission from the publisher. It is illegal to copy this book, post it to a website, or distribute it by any other means without permission.

This novel is entirely a work of fiction. The names, characters and incidents portrayed in it are the work of the author's imagination. Any resemblance to actual persons, living or dead, events or localities is entirely coincidental.

Designations used by companies to distinguish their products are often claimed as trademarks. All brand names and product names used in this book and on its cover are trade names, service marks, trademarks and registered trademarks of their respective owners. The publishers and the book are not associated with any product or vendor mentioned in this book. None of the companies referenced within the book have endorsed the book.

No portion of this book may be reproduced in any form without written permission from the publisher or author, except as permitted by U.S. copyright law.

To Auntie Grace, J.B., and all of the other strong, beautiful, silver-haired women who roar. I see you.

CONTENTS

One	1
Two	12
Three	26
Four	34
Five	48
Six	58
Seven	72
Eight	81
Nine	89
Ten	96
Eleven	112
Twelve	117
Thirteen	126
Fourteen	131
Fifteen	143

Sixteen	150
Seventeen	160
Eighteen	163
Nineteen	169
Twenty	172
Epilogue	177
Also By Tana	181
Acknowledgements	183
About the Author	185

ONE

Devil's Night, Present

The wolf shook his coat and then lowered his nose back to the ground. Exhaustion enveloped him like a dark cloud as he stalked his quarry through the night. He trod on, relentless, shifting his position but never his target. The fate of his pack rested on him, and he'd come too far to give up.

He'd dodged the steel traps of sportsmen and the sharp eyes of his enemies, swapped his familiar mountains for strange hills, crept from the pine forest, trading the soft earth of damp scrub needles for the jagged maze of corn stalks—some of which now lay broken beneath his blistered paws. He'd soldiered on for days, with little water and no food until, at last, he found himself in this foreign field, where thick sheets of icy rain penetrated his coat, chilling him to the bone. And only the tingling heat of his focus, laser-sharp, kept him from shivering.

A bolt of lightning slashed the sky, painting the night a blinding white and toppling a nearby tree with a sizzling crack. He leapt out of the way, panting as he landed on all fours. As he did, he sensed the presence of an unfamiliar wolf lurking in the area, no doubt drawn by the same thing as him. He must be close.

His ears twitched, and his gait stiffened.

Nearby, the racing heart of a rabbit, crouched and hiding, beat fast against its ribcage. The musk of a doe mingled with the wind, tickling the wolf's nostrils. His lips curled and his tongue salivated, the scent of prey thrumming his pulse. Normally, his hunger turned him into a machine. Tonight, he restrained himself.

A wolf was nothing if he couldn't control his urges.

Lifting his snout, he sniffed the cold October air. He took two, then three steps more.

He stopped again. The tension in his haunches uncoiled.

He'd finally found her. She was asleep in the old farmhouse across the empty road. He could almost smell her dreams. Dreams she'd been dreaming for far too long. It was time to wrench her from them, willing or not. His hunger would at last be satisfied.

***

June Chambray bolted upright in her bed.

Something was wrong. Deeply wrong. Every nerve and muscle in her body clenched taut beneath sweat-dampened skin as the fear of death screeched through her.

Instinct had thrust her arm to the other side of the mattress and a mournful groan escaped her lips as she grasped nothing more than cold sheets. Old habits never truly died, even after all this time.

She cast the thought aside to face whatever menace had ripped her from sleep. With their preternatural hearing, her ears strained against the *rat-a-tat-tat* of rain beating the roof, and amidst the rhythm she picked up an echo reverberating from the front door. Yes, there had been a thud. Not a dream thud, but a real thud. Of that, she was certain. The deep, spectral sound had set her stubborn heart galloping, pushed jagged breaths from her anxious lungs, and thrown her head from the pillow.

Aza, her daughter, would no doubt say this was a paranoid hallucination, yet another symptom of the dementia she was convinced was slowly swallowing June's mind.

But her old bones knew better.

Downstairs, a floorboard creaked in the living room of what should have been an empty house. She said a silent curse. That was proof she could have lived without. In her authorial days, this would have made a great start to a horror story, but this was not the work of her imagination, and there was nothing great about another unsettling sound.

Her startled gaze swept the pitch-black room. Blood-red lights glowing on the small bedside table read three a.m. It couldn't be Aza. Her daughter often dropped by unannounced, but never at this ungodly hour.

"Hello? Who's there?" June called, her voice solid, despite the tremor wracking her knees.

Silence answered.

Realizing she'd pulled the quilt to her chest as if it might offer some protection, she let it go and forced herself to inch toward the mattress's edge. A sour odor clung to the walls, one she recognized immediately—her own fear. Although decades had passed since she last grimaced at the stench, the smell, like the situation that had prompted it all those years ago, remained deeply etched in her memory and refused to fade. The accompanying feeling was the same too, like all of her senses had been amplified, and she was doing a deadly dance on the sharp edge of a thin wall keeping two worlds from colliding.

Pressing her lips firmly together, she exhaled through her nose to push the chaotic jumble of sleep and fear into more ordered thoughts. If that moment from her youth had taught her one lesson, it was that panicking over threats—real or imagined—would not lead her to a solution.

Besides, old houses, like old women, made noise as they saw fit. And though June recognized the sounds probably weren't from the house itself, they were likely just as innocuous.

At least that's what she needed to believe to keep moving.

Thin curtains at her bedside whispered softly as she pulled them back, squinting out of the cold dark window to see if anything appeared amiss in the yard below. A fresh shudder threatened, and she cut it off. "We are not having fear or sadness for breakfast today," she told the worried reflection staring back at her. Nor would she allow either of them to feast on her.

She focused her sharp gaze. Rain drummed against the glass panes and thick mists of fog swirled through fields of withered corn stalks. Apart from the tempest, the night was still. Although the grumble of what must have been an engine drifted down the road. She cocked her chin. A faint line of confusion etched her brows. The rumble sounded like the low growl of an angry animal, and no headlights broke the fog...

She shook her head, chastising her imagination like a pesky lapdog. Was she trying to prove her daughter right? No animal was responsible for that sound. Only one explanation made sense.

The paperwoman.

She'd been one of June's English students right before retirement, almost thirty years ago. On the most cheerful of sunny days, she threw the bundle from the car. No doubt she was driving off after doing the same tonight. No one else would be out at this time, especially in this weather.

Storms had been battering the countryside, drowning out all but June's very own thoughts, for days. Nights, too, though she was long accustomed to only keeping time from cockcrow to dusk. Night fell outside of time. Night was that point when she felt all of life most acutely, when her world could be defined most clearly by a solitary word—pain. So night was the period June tried to blot from memory each morning. Thus, the counting of days. As she had been doing for the last fourteen hundred and fifty-nine.

Since George vanished into the gloaming.

June let the curtains fall closed. Not bothering to change out of her ankle-length white nightgown, she pressed her fingers to the cross hanging above the doorway, walked past the desk with the long abandoned manuscript resting atop, and ambled down the stairs to fetch what she had decided could be one thing only—the paper.

Unless...

Holding her breath, she slammed back the deadbolt on the front door. It snapped into place with an angry crack. The noise pierced the rain's heavy staccato, which grew louder as she yanked open the door. But the rain wasn't loud enough to cover the rusty screech of hinges crying out under the weight of centuries-old wood or the sound of June's disappointment—that was deafening in her head. A banshee's wail in the unique key of a shattered heart breaking anew.

For no one stood on the other side. Nothing but the covered porch, big enough to have its own zip code, awaited her.

Frosty, wet winds slapped her face as she stepped onto the porch, exhaling a white cloud. She scanned the area for the newspaper, but the telltale blue package was nowhere to be seen. What, then, made the sounds? Had a crow slammed into the window?

Overhead, the dim, yellow bulb of the porch light buzzed and flickered, casting an eerie glow on the two rocking chairs close to the door. George had made them with his bare hands, using branches from the sugar pines in the woods behind the house. The empty chairs rolled back and forth, as if occupied by drowsy ghosts.

She let go of both a long sigh and her hope of finding him there to greet her. "That would have been too easy, eh, my love? Showing up after all these years on a dark and stormy night to say..."

To say what? She couldn't finish that story, and it had nothing to do with the writer's block that had been trailing her since he'd left. Apart from the strangeness of the sound of her own voice, she simply couldn't imagine what explanation George would have for vanishing, but that he would come with one, she was sure.

She shook her head, trying to solder the old wound with denial. One question at a time. Right now, she wanted to know what, or who, was out there.

Stubborn curiosity hastened her move forward, even as her daughter's doubts about June's sanity circled the edge of her thoughts. She resisted them, along with the terrified impulse to bolt back inside and lock the door behind her, clinging instead to the belief that no lasting harm would befall her until she'd satisfied what had become her life's singular purpose—finding her long-lost husband.

Besides, ghosts did not exist. On the off chance they did, any ghosts that found themselves in these particular chairs were of the Casper variety—harmless.

Right?

She looked at them again to be sure. All she saw was a glimmer of the past.

"Have a seat, my love," George had said, the memory of their first month of marriage crisp in her mind. "We're going to watch every sunset and sunrise for the rest of our lives from these."

True to his word, for sixty-eight years, the creaking sound of the rockers was their lullaby as they watched the sun set on the cornfields and treetops of Central Valley, Ohio. They both loved those golden fields that stretched to the horizon, especially in the winter when the sun routinely disappeared for weeks, and their color was not just a reminder of its warmth, but of the bounty it provided.

Now, as she turned away from the chairs, the fear blinking her eyes made it hard to make out much of anything. She tried to focus on the corn through the rain and dense fog across the road, but her valiant attempts at courage were faltering. She could hear George chiding her, "You have nothing to be afraid of here, my beautiful bride. I will protect you."

And though he'd been gone for some time, she felt his protective embrace as she thought of him. To be afraid would mean she had stopped believing in the power of him, in the power of their love, or the inevitability of his return. And let them call her crazy—relinquishing faith in George was something she would never do.

Scraping wood drew June's attention back to the rocking chairs. They were moving more quickly now. As if her imaginary ghost pair had awoken, excited for something to come.

All at once, the beating rain stopped, the chairs stilled, and the flickering porch light died, leaving her shrouded in darkness.

Her already achy chest tightened. Searching for light, her eyes darted to the porch ceiling and then beyond, where the thick wall of gray clouds split, revealing a jeweled strip of early morning stars—the Milky Way—whiter and fatter than she'd ever seen it before. The celestial river, known to ancient Egyptians as Bat, the fertility goddess, twinkled and glowed so bright, it appeared almost close enough to touch.

June stepped to the edge of the porch to get a better view. The strangeness of the night had her half expecting to see something fantastical like a hovering spaceship. To test the soundness of her reality, she held her palms flat, in mirror to the sky. Lunar rays she could feel rather than see lit her skin. They kneaded her scalp, easing some of her tension.

June inhaled, then choked out a nervous exhale as a buzzing sensation crawled up her neck. Was she being watched?

The nearest neighbors lived miles away. The town was even farther. Most didn't know the remote house existed, surrounded as it was by cornfields on three sides and the pine forest out back. People rarely came out this way. She peered into the corn for the source of the strange sensation, and her ears saw for her. To the right and across the road, a light breeze sent a smattering of tree branches swaying. Leaves cascaded to the damp ground. Corn stalks hissed. Otherwise, the road was silent in both directions.

Determined to test fate no further, she turned to go back inside. As she did, a large shadow hovering, then disappearing near the mailbox, caught her eye. Her pulse cartwheeled. Squinting into the mist again, she made out a small rise that wasn't in the grass yesterday. Was it debris blown by the storm?

June scarcely registered the fog or the wet cold on her bare feet as she crept down the rain-slickened steps. She inched further away from the house until finally, her toes met the road.

There, glinting and motionless, lay the blue plastic bag. June couldn't remember the last time her paper had been left anywhere but leaning against the rocking chair. There was no way the package could have bounced forty feet, and the Sunday edition was far too heavy to blow, even in these winds.

"How on earth did you get all the way here?" she muttered.

Two thoughts struck her like a thunderbolt: someone had knocked on her door, and that someone likely moved the paper, luring her away from the safety of her home.

Bending down to retrieve it, her long white braid fell over her shoulder, and she almost jumped out of her skin at the light brush. Standing, June peeled back a bit of the wet plastic to peer at the contents. The paper whispered beneath her fingers as she ran them across the surface. It was still dry. All was right with the world. Not that she normally did much with the papers herself, but George preferred them crisp.

A howling wind whistled up the empty road, a portent of danger. June went still as a statue. She should have stayed in the house. The biting cold pressed her soft, cotton nightgown against the skin of her hips, arms, and chest.

That was when she felt it—dampness on her bosom, as if her heart were weeping through her skin.

Eyes falling, June marveled at the sight of moisture blooming up like roses on the stem. Her lungs squeezed. She clutched her wet gown and all at once the world imploded. Years of swallowing back emotion—brutal loss compounded by the indignities of aging, laced with fear, oh, so much fear—crystallized by the emptiness, the shadows, and the strange happenings of this night, enveloped her with crushing force.

It wasn't until the last note that June realized she was screaming—a long, shrill piercing sound, quite like the one she'd uttered all those years ago.

At ninety-four years old, June Chambray was lactating.

And as June looked up from her sopping chest, her gaze locked with two golden orbs glowing in the corn. They were quite possibly the eyes of a killer, staring her down, nearly identical to the eyes she'd seen the day she met George.

TWO

Devil's Night, 1949

The last rays of sunshine filtering in through the main window of Peoples' Grocery were June's signal, and she was glad. It had been a long, strange day.

She flipped the switch on her father's 1948 Bendix radio, handling it as carefully as fine china. The dust jacket, one of the final pieces sewn by her mother, came next. June slipped it over the sides of the gleaming wood.

Far as she knew, the portable in her father's five and dime was one of the first ever purchased in their small Colored town, Mt. Hope. Established in the 1800s by runaway slaves and free Blacks, Calvin Moss, her dear adoptive father, tried to make sure the community stayed on top of all of the latest technology. Bought less than a year ago, he loved the music machine almost as much as he loved her—so June always gave it the white glove treatment. But today's focus was especially keen. The result of an afternoon spent desperately searching for a suitable mental anchor, anything to keep her mind off the store's *newest addition*. Of all days to forget a book.

June smoothed the sides of the radio cover into place. As her fingers glided along the area near the base, the box began humming. Seconds later, the muffled broadcast of a ballgame filtered through the static and cloth.

June's chin thrust back. Hadn't she just turned the radio off?

As she lifted the cover, the box fell silent. She peered at the dark face of the machine. The power dial was in the off position and the sound dead.

Shaking her head, she slid the cover back down. Strange day indeed. Maybe she'd just imagined the noise?

"I'm closing up now," she called out.

"Quittin' time already?" a man responded. And June wished she'd only imagined its impact.

His deep, smoky voice made her melt into the realization that her quest for a suitable anchor wasn't over yet. Not by a long shot.

"Yes. You can just finish unloading that crate and head on out," she answered, grabbing two deposit bags for the register and looking away quickly, embarrassed by her tone. Her words had sounded labored, slower than normal, and full of that dreaminess she was always teased about by those who knew her well.

Her altered state was silly, and she knew it. George was just the shy new guy in town. He was nobody to get excited about.

Rather, he was nobody she *wanted* to get excited about, she thought, pulling the pencil and financial diary from the counter drawer. The problem was, she'd noticed him—strong, silent, and handsome—the second she stepped into the store today, before her father had even introduced them. His eyes especially stood out to her: one cornflower blue, the other emerald green. She'd seen nothing more startling or majestic in her life, reminding her of turquoise lagoons in faraway places she read about and hoped to visit one day.

And no matter how hard she'd tried to focus on other things, like the radio, ringing up her customers with their tidbits of gossip and news, or life passing by on the other side of the store's big picture window, a part of her mind had been distracted by his presence all afternoon.

June fingered the small gold badge on her breast. Given to her by Jeffrey Millner, she'd been wearing it proudly for the last two years, since she was eighteen. His father owned the shoe store up the block. Now that she was twenty, and he was back from college, a ring would come soon.

Jeffrey had what her father called "promise." The type of boy her adoptive mother, Clara, had been grooming her to marry since June learned to curtsy at five years old. What's more, his pin had finally made her place in the community feel secure. Overnight, she'd gone from adopted outcast who always had her nose in a book to the girl people envied.

"I'll wait for you," George said, interrupting her thoughts and sending her chin whirling back in the direction of the storeroom on the other side of the narrow store. His broad shoulders nearly filled the doorframe as he leaned against it.

"If you don't mind," he added, tucking one of his massive thumbs into the pocket of his single creased slacks.

Her eyes fell to his full lips with their bowtie center as he spoke. These were the first complete sentences she'd heard from him all day. June, who considered herself a decent study of people, got the impression George didn't talk much. Other than "yes sir," when speaking to her father, she hadn't heard him say anything else. It was probably a good thing. The sound of his voice, sliding like silk over those perfect lips, made her chest rumble and her nerves sizzle even more than they did when she was simply looking at him.

She stepped to the door and turned the sign from open to closed. "That's alright, I'll be fine."

"I'd feel better if you'd let me walk you home, Miss June. It's not safe for you to walk by yourself."

June's hand and hip found each other, her eyes quickly sweeping the quiet dirt road in front of the shop. "Now, that's a funny thing to say. Nothing interesting ever happens around these parts."

Except you, June thought, immediately chastising herself for doing so. Sometimes, she swore her brain had a mind of its own.

Flustered, she yanked the lever on the side of the cash register. It stuck. She yanked it again with a little more muscle, but the drawer still didn't pop open.

See, that's what you get for being distracted.

George crossed from the storeroom with quiet confidence and a quickness June wouldn't have thought possible for someone of his size. Stopping so close she could smell his woodsy and spicy scent mixing with the ripe fall apples on the stand nearby, he reminded her of something she might like to taste. The steamy thought sent heat blasting through her body. She bit her lip, hoping the pain might help her control her reaction.

He toggled the lever; his movements delicate, also surprising given the largeness of his hands. The drawer sprang open. He shrugged shyly, and June smiled back, trying hard not to stare at those beautiful eyes taking her in.

"I think interesting things are always happening in life. Just have to look closely," he continued. His heated gaze made her blush anew and almost wonder if he was suggesting she was one of those 'interesting things' in life.

Not likely.

If dreaming were an Olympic sport, she could win a medal.

Still, June wanted to hear more, wanted to see the world through his mysterious gaze. But when her hip bones hit the counter, she caught herself leaning toward him and jerked back. Shame and attraction mixed inside of her like vinegar and milk, twisting her stomach into knots. What had gotten into her?

"Maybe so, but my fella is going to walk me home," she said, guilt crisping the edges of her words, as she crossed her arms.

His eyes followed her defensive movement and one brow rose. There was a twinkle of amusement in his expression. "Your fella, eh? Hmm. Well, alright, since you've already got an escort...this evening."

Is he implying that Jeffrey is temporary?

"Tomorrow then." George's tone was neutral, his multi-colored gaze anything but—lingering long enough to make June's heart race.

"Hmph," was all June could manage. Hot and cold torrents of conflicting emotions threatened to drown her, so she scooped a handful of coins from the drawer and focused her attention on tallying, effectively ending their little talk. George returned to the storeroom just off the main shopping floor, and though she couldn't see his face, she was sure he was smiling.

When June finally found the courage to lift her chin, she wished she hadn't. The sight of his broad shoulders flexing and stretching the fabric of his shirt as he lifted bottle after bottle from the crates, placing them on their respective shelves, was mesmerisingly seductive. He was a quick worker. June had already noticed that throughout the day, but he took his time emptying the last crate, prolonging her agony.

Tinkling door chimes announced Jeffrey's arrival. Dapper in his three-piece wool suit and trench coat, he had the confident stride that came from being one of the most sought-after boys in Callaloosa County. He flashed June a megawatt smile brighter than the polished tops of his oxfords, and she exhaled, grateful for a reprieve from her troubling thoughts.

"Hi, Jeffrey," she said, smiling.

"Hiya, Junie. You're not ready yet?" His smile darkened. "You'd think after a year of accounting classes at junior college you'd be a little quicker with the books." Frowning, he unfastened the top button of his coat. "You weren't lost in one of your dreaming fits again, were you?"

June looked at the wall on the clock. Never mind that she'd hated those classes and had wanted to study English instead, it was seven p.m. on the dot. The store had been closing at the same time, six nights a week, since it'd opened ten years ago—but somehow, the chap who remembered the shoe size of every man, woman, and child in town always seemed to forget this fact. "I'll hurry. I'm almost finished sorting today's cash."

"Good girl." Jeffrey leaned, giving her a peck on the cheek.

"I see your escort has arrived."

June's gaze snapped in the storeroom's direction where George stood.

Jeffrey's eyes followed hers, and his jaw clenched. "Who's that?" he asked, his tone a challenge.

George strolled out from the storeroom. The power in his gait reminded June of the valiant horse Abraham Galloway rode in the town square sculpture.

A good six inches taller than Jeffrey, George's shoulders were almost twice as broad. And something in his movements told her his muscles resulted from more than hard work. What exactly? June couldn't be sure. But she thought it might be connected to the gleam in his eye, so sharp that Jeffrey dropped his gaze momentarily.

Stunned, June's eyebrows shot up. Normally, Jeffrey's square-jawed good looks, and, of course, his moneyed parentage, were enough to control the room. For the first time that June had seen, he seemed to be eclipsed. She suspected Jeffrey had also noticed the shadow falling over him, literally, as well as figuratively.

June shifted uncomfortably, guilt flushing her cheeks. She'd been itemizing their differences with more positives falling in the George category than the Jeffrey column.

"This is my father's new hire. George, ah, I'm sorry, I didn't catch your last name," she said, looking up at him.

Lips upturned into a friendly smile, George swung his hand toward Jeffrey. "Chambray. George Chambray."

Scowling, Jeffrey took George's much larger hand. "Last name sounds French. You're not from around here, are you?"

"No," George said simply, letting go of the other man's hand. Clearly, he'd taken Jeffrey's dirty look as an exemption from the polite need to explain.

"I thought Jerry Wilkers was looking for work?" Jeffrey said to her. "Why didn't your pops give a local boy the job?"

George's face remained impassive, but a flash of irritation made June's lips twitch.

"Jerry Wilkers?" she asked. That man was a wife beater, the *not-so-secret* secret of their small town. Jeffrey knew it, June knew it, and her father knew it. The comment shouldn't have been made in any circumstances, but especially in front of George, as it was clearly designed to make him feel unwelcome.

"Take care of your own and all." Jeffrey shrugged, like he hadn't just said something offensive.

June gripped the pencil in her hand. A sudden protectiveness made her want to speak up on George's behalf, but the small voice in her head warned it would cause a row, the likes of which would set the small town's gossiping tongues wagging. Even though no one but them would be there to hear it, in Mt. Hope, anything resembling a lover's quarrel always seemed to leak through the walls and circulate like embers in a fire. With her mother's illness, she couldn't chance bringing her parents any more stress than they were already experiencing.

In the end, it didn't matter. George saved her from answering.

"Seems to me that since Mr. Freeman was the one to hire me, he'd be the one you should put that question to. Wouldn't you agree, Jeffrey?" The corners of George's eyes crinkled into a smile that didn't quite match the tone of his voice. He wasn't asking a question, so much as he was giving an order.

For one stunned second, Jeffrey seemed speechless. He tucked his chin and ran his hand over his smooth jaw. "Well now, I suppose you just might have a point there, George. Maybe I'll have to have a little chat with him tonight, when I drop off my girl."

He clearly meant it as a threat of sorts, but George's strange eyes remained unreadable, until he inclined his head toward June, and their gazes met. "I'll see you tomorrow, Miss June." There was a hint of tenderness in his expression, a promise in his words, and an unspoken implication that nothing Jeffrey said would keep him from her. A flood of passion coursed through her, pushing her brows to her hairline, and her gaze shot to Jeffrey. He was busy flicking lint from his trousers. For the first time in her life, she was grateful for the self-centeredness that limited the depth of Jeffrey's observations of others.

"See you tomorrow," she replied, as he drifted toward the door.

"Something's not right about that fellow."

June sucked in a quick breath. Had Jeffrey noticed, after all?

"Did you see his eyes?" he asked.

June winced, sure George had heard the insult. Though if he had, he hadn't paused before his exit. "He seems alright to me." She did her best to make the words light and airy in the hopes they'd evaporate quickly, along with the tension coiling in her chest.

Jeffrey raised his left eyebrow. No doubt he was as surprised as her that she'd spoken up. She'd made an art of mirroring his opinions. On good days, he called her his little parakeet for the way she always singsonged her agreement with him.

"Never seen a Colored man with eyes like that before in my life." Jeffrey snagged a shiny red apple from the stand near the register and polished it on his coat sleeve. It was a habit that annoyed her, mostly because he always tossed them after a few bites.

"Must be some kind of birth defect." Jeffrey bit into the apple and continued talking around the juicy chunks, a few small flecks flying as he spoke. A piece stuck between his bottom molar and he fished it out with his index finger. "He's big, probably dumb too. A bit of trash blown out from the East. Your father should be careful who he lets around such a precious jewel." Jeffrey brushed June's cheek with his damp pointer.

June forced herself not to recoil, but the superior tone he'd taken in talking about her father made her mouth pop open again. "Daddy is a firm believer in hunches. I'm sure he had a good one before he made the hire."

Worried that she'd pressed her luck too far, June dipped her head and reached into the register drawer for the last of the cash. She'd lost track of her tally and concentrated on paying more attention to sorting the day's sales. The larger bag was for the safe. The smaller, a palm full of coin, she would take home to her father. It heartened her to see that even though the earnings were meager, by tomorrow they would have enough for her mother's weekly medicines.

"I don't know. A man's hunches can do funny things when his priorities are challenged. Your mother's illness may be distracting him." Jeffrey took a second bite from the apple, then tossed it into the near-empty waste basket beside the counter.

Out of the corner of her eye, June watched the half-eaten apple roll to a stop in the middle of the bin, all the while fighting the urge to scoop it up. Until recently, her mother was diligent about bringing home the partially rotted fruit and vegetables for their own kitchen table. What they didn't use went to the church. Several people in town wished they had the money to buy even one apple to split with family, let alone to eat themselves.

"Excuse me," she said. Finished with her tallying, June carried the larger bag to the safe in the back room.

"I'm gonna keep my eye on this Georgie fellow," Jeffrey called out, interrupting her as she listened for the small clicks of the dial before unlatching the lock. "I just may have that talk with your father. I'm not sure I like the idea of my gal being alone with some boob all day."

A wife beater is okay, but a hardworking stranger is a problem?

Anger pricked June's forehead. Her temper was starting to peak, and she had to get hold of herself. Jeffrey was clearly intimidated by George, and it had him seeing green. That was probably a common reaction. A man as beautiful as him was likely to intimidate men and women alike. Maybe Jeffrey was right to be defensive. He was probably picking up on her terrible thoughts.

June *tsked* herself as she closed the safe's door. Loyalty went both ways and started with giving your loved ones the benefit of the doubt. Surely, a few off-color remarks weren't grounds to begin condemning your intended. "You have nothing to worry about, Jeffrey Millner," she finally said, returning from the safe.

Jeffrey puffed his chest out. "Of course, I have nothing to worry about! But people talk."

June stuffed the small bag of daily proceeds into her purse and grabbed her coat from the rack. "Let them talk. We know the truth." She winked playfully at Jeffrey.

As June slipped one arm into her jacket, Jeffrey grabbed it. Hard. "Opinions matter. Talk like that can affect business. As the future Mrs. Millner, I thought you would understand."

June grimaced as Jeffrey's fingertips dug into her skin. "Of course, darling. What was I thinking?" June smiled, hoping it, along with her words, would be enough to disarm him into easing his painful grip.

"Don't patronize me, doll!" His jaw tensed.

Jeffrey had gotten gruff before, but manhandling was new—and this new development made her bottom lip quiver with so much force her voice disappeared.

Jeffrey squeezed harder. "Are we clear?"

Her skin pinched and burned under his fingers. A scream clawed the back of her throat, but the chorus of voices from her mother, the preacher's wife, and nearly every woman she'd ever known sang out in her mind, "*A lady never loses her temper in public.*" And if Clara Moss had taught her anything, it was to always comport herself as a lady.

Not sure if she was trying to smooth the situation for herself or him, June forced herself to kiss Jeffrey's cheek. "Crystal clear."

His grip loosened, leaving red marks that would no doubt turn blue by tomorrow. "If you don't talk to your father, I will."

Hadn't he said he was going to do that?

"I'll talk to him tonight," she said, rubbing her arm, wishing she'd have the nerve to speak her mind freely about what just happened. She shrugged on her jacket the rest of the way and opened the door.

"That's my girl." Jeffrey leaned down and kissed her on the forehead as if nothing had happened between them.

THREE

Devil's Night, 1949

By the time they stepped onto the sidewalk, the streetlamps had come on. Other shopkeepers had already closed up for the night. June's father's store was always one of the last to shutter in order to accommodate those needing items on the way home from a day's work at the nearby iron foundry.

"We've got the sidewalk to ourselves," Jeffrey said, taking her hand.

"I see." June tried to follow Jeffrey's lead, to let the past go and relax at his touch, but a slow-burning anger in her chest wouldn't allow it. She dropped his hand, pretending a need to adjust her purse strap on her shoulder. He'd crossed a line. Her body had gone into danger mode. Her cells were a small army, each one at attention and on the lookout for the next jab from him.

Her gait slowed as he continued around the next corner, oblivious, and she thought back to Jerry Wilkers's wife—*how long was Alice with Jerry before his true colors came out?*

Suddenly, her ears pricked at the steady thud of footfall behind her. As the steps drew nearer, June cast her chin over her shoulder. An enormous man, almost as big as George, dressed all in black, lunged at her with the speed of a bullet. She gasped and somehow managed to dodge him.

"Get away from me," she said, stepping back.

"That's not happening."

His size alone was intimidating, but what scared her breathless was the glow in his yellow eyes. He looked inhuman.

"We'll see about that." Thankfully, her words didn't match the fear roiling inside. *Where was Jeffrey?*

The man chuckled and reached for her, his gloved hand grasping her shoulder. "Feisty. I like it."

The word had never been used to describe her before. 'Mousy' was far more familiar, but darned if there wasn't a first time for everything. "Get your hands off me." She gripped her purse, trying to protect the contents from this thief, as she wriggled out of his firm grip. "Jeffrey!" she called.

"Do you really think that *child* can help you?" He yanked her arm again.

She yanked back. Maybe Jeffrey wouldn't, but there was no way she'd let this deranged ogre come between her and her mother's medicine. Though she'd never been a fighter, it seemed some things were hard-wired. June's mother would give her life for her and June would reciprocate with nothing less.

His vice-like grip tightened, and she yelped, twisting her arm and body, struggling to get loose. Her bun came undone, and her curls tumbled untamed around her shoulders. She'd spent twenty minutes securing them this morning; free now, a wildness fell over her that was at once frightening and exhilarating as she fought to protect what was hers.

In her excitement, she stumbled, giving her opponent an opportunity to get his second bear-sized hand around her other arm. He clutched the same tender bicep Jeffrey had gripped moments ago. She jerked, each movement sending double pain bolting into her shoulder and elbow.

They lurched back and forth. Her purse strap snapped and sheer panic spread through her as her bag fell to the ground. When the thief's eyes didn't follow, instead remaining locked on her, the shock of realization clapped like thunder—his interest lay not in the purse, but in her.

She'd had it all wrong. A fresh round of panic shot through her.

He wasn't a thief; he was something much, much worse. Again, she wanted to scream for Jeffrey, but there was no time and she was surer than she'd ever been about anything in her life—if she didn't fight with everything she had, she'd die in more ways than one.

She flailed about faster now, anger with her situation strengthening her movements. Furious, June lifted her knee, kicking the man in his shin with the point of her hard-toed spectators. A loud crack, like bones breaking, ricocheted through the empty street.

The huge man grunted, and his eyes rounded, clearly surprised at the power behind her kick. Jeffrey finally returned. June realized what felt like hours to her was only seconds. "Take your hands off her!" Jeffrey spat out.

Ignoring Jeffrey, the man swung at June. Ducking just in time, her chin narrowly avoided his knuckles. June kicked again. This time, her wooden heel landed squarely in the man's chest. Rubbing the area, he smiled, a slow, sick smile. "I knew you'd be strong, little witch wolf, but this is a surprise."

Witch wolf?

Then, to her utter bafflement, the man stuck out his tongue as if tasting the air, and, strange as it was, she knew exactly why. She'd smelled the sour scent herself—fear seeping from her pores. Mouth agape, June watched as he licked his lips and moaned in pleasure. She swallowed back her revulsion.

Jeffrey balled his fists, then lifted them in a boxing pose. "I said unhand her!"

The man laughed, a deep sinister cackle that iced her spine and stopped her in her tracks. Several seconds passed during which she couldn't move, the ghoulish sound cementing her in place.

An awful crack snapped the air, releasing June from her shock. The man had punched Jeffrey in the jaw. Before she could do anything, Jeffrey dropped unconscious on the ground with a miserable thunk that made June's own back hurt.

"What have you done?" She lunged toward Jeffrey, but the man grabbed her waist, preventing her from reaching him.

Turning quickly, he closed his other arm around her back, and in seconds, she was like a fish in a net. Her attacker's thick biceps tightened and held her arms pinned as he hoisted her over his shoulder with no more effort than one would lift a pillow.

"Let me go, you pig! I said unhand me this minute!"

What was she doing? Talking to this brute made no sense. Clearly, he had no intention of heeding her pleas.

"Help!" June screamed, terrified, praying that someone, anyone, in the town's commercial area would hear. "Help! Help!"

Unfazed, the man took a few running steps, and as he spirited her away, the world blurred into one gigantic ball of fuzz.

In seconds, railroad tracks replaced the sidewalk. By the time June had emptied her lungs of her first scream, he'd somehow dragged her all the way to the shadows on the edge of town. Dazed, June shook her head. Had she fainted? No one could run that quickly.

She kicked the air. "Let me down!"

All at once, he slung her off his shoulder and she stumbled when her feet hit the ground. Knees jellied, her legs collapsed underneath her. In one swift movement, he bound her wrists using a thin metal chain, similar to a necklace. Appearing entirely too weak to contain her, she yanked, but the links remained secure. She tried to hit the man with both hands. Not only did the odd links prevent her from punching him, it was as if all the anger and rage she felt flowed in reverse, into her. Her body ached from it.

The man's face split into a gruesome grin. Her pain delighted him. Was this what abject terror felt like? A powerful monster punching the guts of your soul?

He crouched over her, his now red eyes gleaming with raw lechery. "You have no idea how hard it's been to find you."

The attack wasn't random? He was looking for me, specifically?

Forget his impossibly changing eyes and attempted theft. *This* was definitely the pinnacle of horror.

Bile scorched the back of her throat, and a second wave of revulsion washed over her as his scent—putrid, rank, and wrong—filled her nostrils. Fear, unlike anything she'd ever known before, turned the world red. Her burning lungs seized in panic. He leaned closer, his long, oily hair tickling her cheek as he pressed his nose to her sweat-soaked forehead and inhaled. Her body stiffened. She needed to get away from him. She could butt his teeth, get enough time to scramble to her feet and run. But no sooner had the thought crossed her mind than he pulled back, his eyes glinting with sheer arousal.

"You smell so good," he said, rubbing his hand along his swollen crotch.

The vile man intended to do the unspeakable. And she feared that was only the beginning.

Tears sprang to her eyes. She willed them not to fall. She refused to give up hope. Today had shown her something. Abandoned at an early age, in many ways, she had been born fighting, and now that she'd tasted her own power, she wasn't going to stop. Hands tied or not, she was going to make sure this man knew he'd picked the wrong woman.

A low growl from the shadows sent both of their chins shooting toward the alley. The man stiffened and crouched, responding with his own low growl. The deadly warning reminded her of the demons Preacher spoke of at Sunday sermons—walking among us, clothed as men. Until today, June had believed Preacher's words to be merely metaphor. Maybe they still were. Maybe fear had her ears mishearing.

The man-beast growled again, hunching and creeping toward the corner that opened into the alley.

He paused, head cocked as if listening for the sound of his enemy, when an enormous claw blasted from the shadows. Petrified, June watched as it caught on the vile man's lapel. She squeezed her eyes shut, scrambling backward, then flipped onto her knees to crawl away as fast as she could. She wasn't sure if he'd been dragged or leaped, but when she opened her eyes, he was gone.

Seconds later, ghastly sounds filled the air, letting her know they were fighting in the alley. June's mind seized on one thought and one thought alone—*Run!*

Forcing herself to her feet, she flew over the railroad tracks and back toward town. Lungs burning, adrenaline soaring, she pushed herself harder than she thought possible. At some point, she pulled her wrists apart, breaking the metal cuffs from them. Once they were removed, the horrible sensation that her body was one gigantic bruise lifted, and June's pace quickened even more.

Turning at the block to her father's shop, her heart nearly jumped out of her throat when her eyes landed on a small group of people: Mr. Hample, Jeffrey, and two deputies.

She was safe.

Or am I?

June didn't know if she'd ever be safe again.

FOUR

Halloween, 1949

The day after the attack, the neighborhood came alive with the song of children's laughter. A boy donned a paper mask, giggles trailing behind him as he chased another who'd tied corn stalks to his limbs and knotted a kerchief around his neck. A group of girls in sheets and tiaras—ghost princesses—skipped rope. Halloween had arrived, gracing Mt. Hope with bright blue skies and a sun that danced through fall leaves. The children couldn't contain their glee.

June sat at the window-side perch in her mother's bedroom, an open book on her lap as the sound of their merriment comforted her like a warm blanket. She gazed out, her thoughts drifting and bittersweet. The bitterness took the form of a quiet dread of her next entry into the world, mixed with an almost painful longing for those undiluted moments of childhood joy. As she watched the children's carefree play, she could scarcely imagine feeling that way again.

The doorbell rang, and her gaze swung to her mother. Clara Moss looked at her apologetically from the bed, obviously upset that *she* couldn't be the one to open the door—to shield her daughter from the world.

A frown tugged at June's mouth, but she refused to give in and pressed her lips together instead. Her mother's reaction pained her. Already sick and bedridden, last night, news of the attack sapped what little energy she had, and she still hadn't recovered. Clearly, she felt she'd failed her daughter, first by getting sick, then by not protecting her from whatever had accosted her last night.

June patted her mother's hand as she stood. "I'll be right back, Mama. I'm sure it's just someone else from the church."

"Take your time, Baby." But the note of worry in her mother's tone begged her not to be gone too long.

There'd been a steady stream of members visiting since last night when the news of her attack first broke. June was surprised. She'd never really felt like she fit in with the townspeople. No doubt, they were stopping by more out of respect for her parents than for her. Still, she appreciated the gestures, if for no other reason than that they hinted at some semblance of normalcy in the world.

Pulling open the door, June's heart danced in her chest and the smile she'd affixed to her face morphed into a solid "O." There stood George with his multi-colored gaze, searching and full of concern.

"Hi June." His husky voice was thunder and it rumbled through every inch of her.

"Hi." Her response was way more breathy than she would have liked. But the man had a larger-than-life quality that nearly spelled her. He towered, even from a step beneath her, and he looked even more handsome than he had the day before. Part of her wondered if she was dreaming.

Another part of her, a part she didn't want to admit existed, eyed him warily. She searched his eyes for shadows and scanned the corners of his smile for falters or cracks that might hint at a lack of sincerity, at danger. Hard as she tried, all she saw was genuine compassion.

"You fancy readin'?" he asked, his voice a slow rolling river of curiosity.

She trailed his gaze to the book still cradled in her hand. "I do." She braced herself for one of the jokes she'd been hearing her whole life.

"That's a mighty fine quality. They say, people who read tend to carry hearts wide and warm as the open road."

She pressed her lips together to keep from smiling like a fool at the sense of validation he inspired. So different from Jeffrey's constant negative commentary on the topic. "Doesn't that all depend on what the pages say?"

He chuckled. "I meant '*usually*.'"

"Fair enough." She held the book between them. "Are you a reader?"

He took it, and their fingers grazed. The light touch nearly imbalanced her, but if anything, it seemed to make him stand taller. "No ma'am. Never learned my letters. Reckon you could be my tutor?"

He was playing a part, teasing her, and his humor glided through her soul like one of T-Bone Walker's guitar riffs on a hot summer night. But her only answer was a narrow-eyed smile. She still wasn't sure how to engage with this man.

"Your hair is different." He swiped his hat from his head, held it with both hands. "You look beautiful."

Beautiful?

June blinked and her hand flew to her S-shaped spirals. She'd hovered for an hour at the mirror this morning as she dressed. Scanning the glass for some vestige of the young woman who'd looked back at her yesterday and, finding nothing, finally accepted she was permanently changed.

Today's style reflected that realization. It was wild and rebellious— but last night, she'd felt such a power when her hair was down and natural. For the first time in her life, she'd owned her anger. She hadn't been focused on pleasing people or battling her reactions to others. She'd felt terrified but also purely alive and strong. Today, more than ever, she needed to harness that power. So instead of pinning it up and slicking it back with one of Madame Walker's proteins, June opted to let her hair hang free, halfway to her waist.

Looking into George's admiring eyes now, she wasn't so sure about the decision. His attention made her feel exposed. At the same time, she knew comfort with vulnerability was part of her path to strength and healing.

"Thank you," she finally said, simply.

George nodded and for an instant, as he held her gaze, she got the sense that he understood every aspect of her internal struggle. For the first time since last night, it felt like someone from the town was truly there for her.

"Your father mentioned an escort to the store. I'm guessin' you're surprised to see me."

"After yesterday, I'm not so sure *surprise* is a word I'll ever use again." She smiled, and George tilted his head, sympathy warming his eyes. It'd been said as a joke, but actually, it was true. June wasn't surprised. Not entirely, at least.

Her father had wanted to keep the store closed today so the family could all stay home together. "Just this one day," he'd said. "We can afford to be closed for one day."

Except they all knew they couldn't. Though yesterday's proceeds had been recovered, the family still needed today's money for her mother's medical expenses. When June insisted her father open the store, he tried to convince her to stay home anyway.

She refused.

There was no advantage in cowering indoors. If she started hiding now, she might never stop and, no matter how shaken she was, June resolved not to live in fear. Before she'd finally convinced him to leave for work that day, he'd agreed to do so only on the condition that someone walk with her. She expected one of the men from First Baptist, but wasn't sure who. Most, like her own father, couldn't afford to take time off of work.

Jeffrey was going to be recuperating for a few days, so he wasn't an option, and he'd be livid if he learned George had been the one to walk her in his absence. In their small town, there was little chance Jeffrey wouldn't hear. And *no* chance of avoiding an argument once he did. *If* she chose to walk with George, that is. Sure, Jeffrey had treated her terribly just before the maniac tried to abduct her, but she was still unsure what to do about his behavior.

Noting her long pause, George inclined his head. "I hope it's okay that I walk you. I know we don't know each other very well. I can understand if you'd like someone else at your side." He ran a hand over his low, tight curls, then gripped the brim of his hat. The move conveyed a gentle patience that set June at ease. He would respect whatever decision she made.

Was George's offer worth tossing away the life she had mapped out with Jeffrey?

"Yes, maybe," June said, the dip between his brows making her realize she'd blurted an answer to the question in her head instead of the one he'd asked aloud. "I mean, no. That won't be necessary. It was kind of you to oblige my father's request, and I would appreciate your escort. Please, won't you step inside?" She turned, motioning for him to enter.

In the foyer of their tidy house, standing so close to George she could almost hear him breathing, June smoothed her moist palms over her skirt. Her own touch was a wake-up call, a rooting to her body. Coursing beneath all of her tumultuous feelings of the last several hours was a deep yearning to see George—an aching need to lay eyes on him, that had begun the moment they parted the evening before. His strong, calming presence, this intense magnetism between them, made any trouble on earth seem manageable.

June's stomach somersaulted as self-consciousness took hold of her. Most normal people didn't develop such potent feelings for folks they'd just met. Especially one who was only there because her father had foisted her upon him. "Sorry, I know you didn't sign up for this when you applied to work at the store," she said uneasily. For all she knew, his talk yesterday had been just that—talk—and he had a woman waiting at home for him.

"I volunteered, June. I'm here because I want to be here and nowhere else."

June nearly gasped. So, his frank expressions of interest had been genuine.

George steadied his gaze on her. It was so powerful, June felt like he could see straight into her soul. "Somehow that doesn't surprise me either." She smiled and held his gaze.

"No, I would hope that it wouldn't." He winked, meeting her bold humor with his own, adding just the right touch of gentleness. She didn't think she could possibly feel any closer to him in that moment—even if he kissed her. And for a second, she thought he might.

"Give me one minute. I'm almost ready." June ran upstairs to tell her mother goodbye, grateful for a break and an opportunity to collect herself. On the way out the door, she grabbed her coat and turned her collar up against the brisk air. Stepping from the bottom step onto the front walk, she looked at George and paused. "You're not wearing a coat?"

He shook his head.

"Let me at least grab you one of my father's scarves. I'm freezing just looking at you." She bit her lip, worrying maybe poverty kept him from warmer clothes and that her comment might somehow embarrass him.

"Really, I promise, it's by choice," George said, grinning down at her as he offered his elbow. June slipped her hand into the crook, his warmth making her gloved fingertips tingle delightfully. "I run hot enough to go barefoot in December."

"Um, too soon for demon jokes," June deadpanned.

George stopped walking, his jeweled eyes suddenly grave with concern. "I didn't mean it like that. It was just an expression, really. I'm so sorry."

June laughed. "I'm just kidding, George. Trying to break the tension." She wanted him to know she wasn't so fragile. The joking also helped to remind her of that fact.

George let out a sigh of relief. "Well done. You had me going there." His face broke back into a huge grin, and June felt her knees get a little shaky. His smile was pure sunshine.

But when they reached the corner, she fell silent. Her safe house suddenly felt far away and dark sentiments clouded her thoughts once again. Briefly, June second-guessed herself and her decision to parade down the street with this virtual stranger. Was she seeing something in George that wasn't really there?

No.

Yesterday had smacked her rose-colored glasses off of her face. The change had been quick, but sometimes trauma was an immediate life changer, with effects showing up right away. She now knew what monsters looked like. June searched George's marble-colored eyes. No monster could fake the tenderness and ferocity she saw gazing back at her. But that didn't change the fact that all morning long little noises or unexpected movements had been triggering flashbacks of the strange man's devilish eyes.

Who is he, and why did he attack me?

"That man isn't going to come back for you, June." George wasn't looking at her but at a Ford sedan crawling up the road. June stood at his side, doing the same, allowing her mind to revisit the moments before she'd run. Neck tensing, she thought of the massive claw that had erupted from the shadows to snatch her attacker. Was it an animal? Given the vicious noises she'd heard, believing it was an animal and that it had destroyed the vile man was easy. Still, she hadn't seen anything after her attacker had been dragged into the alley. Terror had kept her from sticking around.

George looked down at her hand around his bicep. Had her fingers clenched him as she recalled the unsettling memory?

"You believe me, but you're still scared, aren't you?" he asked, his voice so full of gentle understanding that she wasn't embarrassed by her display of fear. He covered her hand with his, briefly, the comforting gesture instantly pushing back some of her concern. "This is the first time in your life you've tasted genuine fear. The world is different for you now. From here on out, you'll mark time by that day. The June before yesterday and the June after."

He was right. And while June appreciated his keen insight, his somber tone piqued her mischievous side. She'd had her fill of seriousness these last two days and couldn't help poking fun at a young man sounding off like a grim, ancient one. "You must think you had an awful large impact, don't you, big fella?"

George laughed. "I wasn't talking about us meeting."

June winked. "Sure you weren't."

"Maybe I shoulda been?" Like a good dance partner, he followed her moves, matched her humor with his own, gave as good as he got, and June liked it. She could never joke back and forth like this with Jeffrey. Their roles were fixed—serious businessman and sweet, little woman—at least in his mind. But with George, she could be funny, sad, scared, strong. George gave her the freedom to be as many versions of herself as she liked, and it felt good.

***

"You know, at some point, you're going to have to stop walking me to the shop. Jeffrey doesn't like it," June said to George Monday afternoon, a week after the attack. They were alone in the store, and George was on a rare ten-minute break. She still hadn't ended things with Jeffrey for good, uncertain about giving up the safe and predictable life she'd been planning for the last few years.

"Do I look like I care about Jeffrey, June?" He smiled. "I care about you, about keeping you safe." He was looking at her with those smoldering blue-green eyes. His response unnerved her so much that she fumbled the cheesecloth in her hand, nearly dropping the shiny red apple she was polishing.

"Look here, let me take care of that for you," he said, sliding a copper penny across the counter. Lifting the apple from her hand, their fingers brushed, his burning hers where they touched, a light fire that sent delicious thrills rippling across her skin. George pulled out a pocketknife and quartered the apple. Pushing two juicy pieces toward her, he brought the third to his mouth, his lips caressed the skin tenderly, lovingly. June couldn't tear her eyes away and felt the fire his touch had ignited, stirring something deep inside of her. "This is the shiniest, sweetest apple I've ever tasted. Thank you."

"Thank you?"

"Are those not the words one uses to convey gratitude and appreciation?" he asked, his tone artificially proper and crisp.

June pressed her lips together. Of course they were, but after years of Jeffrey taking like the world belonged to him, George's gratitude nearly struck her dumb. He was grateful, and June adored him for it, which he clearly found joke-worthy.

They finished the day without returning to that topic, and a week later, George was still escorting June to work. She looked forward to those daily walks. They'd gotten comfortable enough with one another that they often made them in companionable silence. Although, it wasn't entirely silent on June's part. She always felt the air thicken whenever George was near. It filled with a pleasant humming she imagined flowed from deep in her bones to his.

Friday night, George asked her to hear some Blues at a makeshift stage near the old cotton gin. As much as she would have loved to, she declined without explanation. He knew, and she knew he knew, her reasons.

"He's not the right one for you, June," George said, breaking their silence and sending the pleasant humming sound into a full roar. "I am."

June looked at him, eyes wide, unsure she'd heard him correctly. She couldn't believe his words. However, what truly shocked her wasn't that he felt them, but that he'd said them aloud. On some level, she'd hoped their unspoken feelings would resolve themselves without a direct conversation. Now that he'd put this thing between them into the light of day, she felt guilty.

A mawkish voice inside her head told her she shouldn't have encouraged such forward behavior from him. "You've only known me for a short time."

"And we both knew it the first second," he said, his voice thick with desire.

June wanted to argue. Love at first sight was a myth. At least that's what she'd always told herself, but she couldn't lie. The pull toward George wouldn't let her. It was its own entity—irrefutable, mesmerizing, even. Her heart answered the call of George's heart, not Jeffrey's. In fact, she wasn't even sure that hers and Jeffrey's had ever been a heart-match. She doubted it had been for him.

These last few weeks with George made her realize that apart from their size, there was another vast difference between George and Jeffrey; Jeffrey got what he wanted using a golden key that had been given to him—his reputation, his identity. It all came from the accomplishments of his father and grandfather, who'd built the small financial fiefdom Jeffrey planned to maintain.

George was the exact opposite. George's respect wasn't given, but earned. A king of kings, his crown wasn't material, it was made of something more valuable and much harder to describe. He had the manner and bearing of one who should control an empire. He was someone people would follow out of respect, plain and simple. He was the one she could trust to never lead her heart astray.

George was the one walking her, comforting her with his strength and presence ever since the attack. George was the one who laughed at her jokes and assured her that everything would be okay. And most of all, George was the one who made her feel things she'd never felt with Jeffrey.

"Not only can I protect you, I can make you strong enough to protect yourself."

She couldn't respond to his bold declarations, nor could she resist the opportunity for a little more humor. "Oh yeah? What have you got in mind, tough guy?"

FIVE

Devil's Night, Present

June dashed into her farmhouse, slamming the door shut behind her and bolting all the locks. Satisfied she was now safe from the danger lurking in the corn, she flew up the stairs to her bedroom, both hands clutching her wet gown. Wet, from milk.

Milk?

She'd sniffed it, tasted it, and knew without a doubt that it was milk. But no matter how many times she said the word over in her mind, she remained in a state of disbelief over the events of this early morning.

Wild animals came and went. That was a terrifying fact of living in an isolated, rural area, especially at 3 o'clock in the morning. But ninety-two-year-old women didn't, couldn't, lactate. It was impossible. That she was now made zero sense. So June did what she always did with things that didn't make sense. She made a mental grab for George's drill.

"Our mind is our toolbox," he'd said, all those years ago, pointing to his head. "You can put anything in it you choose. Anything, June. The sky's the limit."

Panic had wracked June's chest that day, making it hard to breathe. Even harder still to speak. With anything being possible, nothing came to mind. Her toolbox, as he'd put it, was empty. "What do *you* use?"

"*Me*?" he asked. "I use a drill." His warm brown cheeks broke into a shy, sexy smile. "A very *big* one."

"Well, when you put it like that, the choice is easy." She'd smiled back.

The trick was old hat now, much loved and frayed around the edges, performed so often she could do it and count backward from ten thousand at the same time. Sometimes she did it without even thinking.

After changing into faded house clothes and padding her ancient bra with folded Kleenex from the bedside table, she stood in the center of their bedroom following the instructions George had taught her seventy-two years before.

June's mind became a metal drill.

Visualizing a massive metal bit, she watched it twist through crust, mantle, and outer and inner core. As soon as the walls of the hole plunged so deep they kissed the earth's blazing red center, she closed her eyes, hurling all thoughts of lactating breasts straight down the seemingly bottomless middle. When she heard her own thoughts finally land with a sizzle, a sure signal for her milk to dry, June opened her eyes and added her own little spin to the lesson George had originally taught.

Holding one hand up and the other down, she imagined herself as a link in an energetic chain between earth and sky. The left hand receiving, the right expelling, she said, "Take my fear and pain and return it as wisdom and understanding." Then June opened her eyes, noted the red glowing lights reading three-thirty a.m. on her bedside clock, recognized she was now too keyed up for sleep, and promptly went back downstairs to get an early start on her day.

At the bottom of the stairs, she glanced through the window at the side of the door. The yard remained empty.

She picked up the newspaper that had started it all. Lately, the newspapers were catalysts for all sorts of change in June's life. Searching her living room for a place to rest the newest one, she sidestepped the front window, which was open and filling the room with a chill. Last night, like every night in the past four years, she'd raised it before going to bed, just enough for a keyless husband to slip his fingers under. Now, a wintry breeze set her white lace curtains billowing, illuminated by the muted moon-glow that washed over her faded sofa, two tattered armchairs, and a once-shiny coffee table.

The same silver glow made it impossible to hide the rest of the room's contents. Even in shadow, their abundance made them a natural focal point.

Newspapers. Hundreds of them.

Jaundice-colored piles leaned like drunken old men against the walls in her living room, a small mountain range of papers creating their own jagged horizon. The result of four years accumulations— a fact her daughter reminded her of repeatedly and with growing intensity, culminating in an epic argument last Sunday and the task she now set about completing.

June held the paper to her chest and shook her head. Aza lived with her husband Hank less than five miles from the family home. Her weekly visits had long been a regular occurrence. During them, June often wondered how she could have given birth to a child so different from either herself or her husband. Not appearance-wise. Straight-backed and lithe, Aza was the mirror of her mother. Both were often mistaken for women half their years.

In fact, it wasn't until her daughter reached an age where lines unquestionably should have etched her smooth features that June understood others' wonder regarding this aspect of her family. Her entire life she'd heard 'Black don't crack.' Her whole family, with their high cheekbones and smooth skin, was living proof. Hank, whose blonde hair had long ago turned to gray, would joke that he'd unknowingly married a woman half his age.

Last Sunday, after a lunch of vegetable soup and cornbread, she and Aza were doing the dishes when her daughter launched the winning salvo in their long-standing war. "If you don't get rid of them, Mother, I will. I will call the town if I have to, report you for hoarding. Have you carried away by the little white men in their little white jackets."

By the next day, June had a change of heart. For years, she'd kept the papers because George had been obsessed with them in the last days. The logical response to her supposition that something in the papers had triggered his disappearance would have been to scour the papers herself. But she hadn't done that.

No, she'd let them pile. As though whatever code they contained could only be cracked by him. Problematic, but not for the reasons that vexed her daughter, she now realized. June's uncharacteristically defeatist thinking, likely attributable to her near-incapacitating sorrow over George's absence, had allowed precious years to race by. In that time, the trail of clues that might lead to her missing husband had grown cold.

Now that the fog of depression was finally lifting, she'd attacked the piles with a vengeance. And even though a week had passed since she'd begun her review, and June still hadn't found what she was looking for—the papers he'd been reading just before his disappearance—her heart skipped each time she looked at an unexamined batch. She clung to the belief that the answer was there, just an arm's length away.

June crossed to the corner of the living room and switched on a table light, placing this morning's paper on a pile tucked between the wall and an armchair. This particular tower, like all the others combed through so far, was useless, coming in the days *after* George's disappearance.

June looked at the three piles left to be examined before her daughter and son-in-law came later this morning to clear them away for good. Each one rose about chest high. She smiled. After going through dozens upon dozens of piles, three was nothing. Today would be the day.

Sliding off the top paper shuffled loose a familiar scent, an odd alchemy of sweet from the yard pine and salt from George's sweaty toil therein—both made stale by the added chemistry of old age. For years before he'd gone, she'd tried to cover the smell with anything she could find, but now, she was grateful she hadn't succeeded.

Chuckling, June took several more papers from the stack closest, together about as thick as ten pizza boxes, and put them on the floor. They were easier to flip through that way.

Scan, toss, scan, toss. That was her system.

June blinked at the sixth paper in her assembly-like process. The date on the top left read November 5th. Six days after George's disappearance. She was so close. Though she knew none of the articles inside triggered his departure, she scanned the headlines. Her brows rose when she came upon an article in the middle of page two.

A child that had gone missing months before George, still hadn't been found. State authorities were perplexed. Did this have anything to do with her husband? It must. No one ever went missing in this area.

An unfamiliar noise, like a guitar pick running slow on a high chord, froze June's review. She turned toward the door, her pulse picking up tempo. The noise came once more. Something or someone was scratching the wood. Holding her breath, she leaned forward, listening as the unnerving sound stopped and started again. The small hairs on her arms pricked and her hands shook as the memory of the earlier thud assaulted her.

Had the lure returned?

Was it the creature with the golden eyes?

Maybe Aza was right. Maybe June was too old to live alone. Or perhaps her mind was no longer as strong as she'd liked to think.

No, she wasn't going to let herself go silly again. If she ignored the sound, surely whatever was making it would go away. June exhaled and returned her attention to the article she was certain would offer valuable clues.

Scratch. Scratch. Scratch.
Scratch. Scratch. Scratch.

A tree branch? No. George had clear-cut the yard shortly after they moved in. He wanted to be sure no trees would come crashing through the roof during a storm, and he didn't like bushes near the door—saying something about people hiding in them.

The soft scratching continued. Nothing near the door would account for such a sound.

Unless....

George.

Anticipation surged through June like a lightning bolt, and she dropped the papers.

A voice inside told her to stay put, but a stronger, deeper, irresistible pull urged her not to let the moment pass.

She pressed her palm to the chair beside her and rose from the floor, fully aware that her actions made no sense. Hadn't she just run inside, scared for her life? Yes. Yet, she was powerless to do anything but put one foot in front of the other, through the living room, and into the large foyer where she stopped to brace her hand against the wall.

She bowed her head. Desperation and loss were a lethal mix.

Earlier this morning she'd raced to the front door full of hope and promise. She didn't dare do that to herself again.

This time, she opened the door slowly, guarding her heart from disappointment. Perhaps that was why she merely gasped when her eyes adjusted to see an enormous dog standing motionless on her porch.

"What on earth?"

Locked in his massive jaw was something small and shiny. A piece of jewelry?

"That's not..." Her voice trailed. George wore a necklace. Was that his? She couldn't be sure, covered as it was in red dirt, which in these parts meant it had been buried deep.

She leaned down to get a closer look.

The animal lowered his ears while looking up at her with round, pleading eyes, golden along the edges. The same orbs she'd seen earlier.

Much larger than any dog she had ever seen, his hair thick, but not matted, June knew what her reaction should be. Knew that she should be frightened, nay terrified, by the sight of what she was gradually realizing was a wolf at her door.

But with this animal, intelligent enough to have summoned her, she was simply curious, and intrigued by the object peeking from his mouth, held in place by his long, pointed canines. She'd heard of pigeons being used to deliver items—wolf delivery was a first.

"What brings you to my doorstep?" she inquired of the beast.

As though he understood her, he cocked his left ear, turned, and drifted down the stairs. Stopping at the bottom, he looked over his shoulder as if making sure that she was following. He adjusted his grip so that whatever was in his mouth dangled now, but June would need to get closer to make it out.

Standing in the doorway, June cast a lingering gaze into her living room, at the paper she'd just stumbled upon. She found herself at a crossroads, torn. She could go back to scouring the scattered papers, or she could follow the wolf. Some would say both paths were paved with sheer madness.

June took one step and then another. By the time she was well into her backyard, she realized the wolf was heading toward the area her daughter used to call the Enchanted Wood. She pressed herself to move faster and jolted when the blast of exhaust blowing out of a rusty tailpipe broke the country silence. It had to be Hank's Ford coming up the road. The wolf must have heard it, too, for he took off in a sprint, but not quickly enough to escape unseen.

"Mama!" Aza jumped out of the pickup, already running to her mother by the time Hank shifted into park.

Before June could answer, shots rang out. The sound of the discharge was enormous. It echoed against every bone in June's body. She spun around to see Hank standing by the side of the truck, the butt of a rifle pressed against his shoulder, scanning the tree line, searching for the wolf.

A second round of shots tore through the air. The world went dark, and June fell to the ground.

SIX

Present

June's eyes blinked open, her gaze shifted from the white ceiling to the curtained windows as the world around her came into slow focus in the late afternoon sun. Soft fabric tickled her neck. Spread over her and tucked under her chin was her mother's antique crochet coverlet from the guest room. She was on the couch in the living room; her surroundings familiar but somehow changed, and other than a dull ache in her tailbone, she felt fine.

But how'd she get here? And what was different in this room?

They cleared the papers! Panic seized her, twisting and dashing her heart as she thought about the November issue she'd held earlier in the day. Something told her they were gone for good.

Over the sound of water running, the muffled words of Hank and Aza's conversation drifted in from the kitchen.

"It's like she thought he was a stray dog or something," Hank said.

"Yeah, it's gotten terrible," Aza answered.

Hank murmured something else, then the back door slammed shut. Aza stepped out of the kitchen, wiping her hands on a dish towel. Seeing her mother's open eyes, she crossed the living room to kneel by her side. Her face hovered just a few feet over June, a blurred mass of furrowed brow and concern. "You're awake."

"What happened?" June asked. But as soon as the question was out, she remembered the blasts that sent icy fear exploding through her veins—a strange fear, one that wasn't entirely her own. Mostly hers, but also...through the haze in her mind she could have sworn some of the terror belonged to the animal.

No, it can't be.

"Mama, what were you thinking? Following after a wolf. And it's practically winter. You didn't even have your shoes on." Aza made a face like her mother had walked through fire instead of simply across cold earth.

"Where's Hank?" June whispered hoarsely.

"In the forest. He went to go find the wolf."

"You mean it got away?" June asked, desperate to hear that the animal hadn't been shot.

Aza seemed to misinterpret her mother's concern. She smoothed out the already smooth blanket. "Don't worry, Mama. Hank will find him. He won't leave until he does."

June let go a short breath. The wolf had escaped. She doubted Hank could catch him, or at least, she prayed he wouldn't. "Call him back. Tell him to leave the wolf alone."

"Hank's a hunter. You know he won't do that."

Hank did whatever Aza demanded. Really, for the millionth time, June wondered how she and her domineering daughter could be so different. But arguing with her was no use. "And the papers?"

"Hank burned them out back. One mess taken care of."

Mess!

Devastation took June's breath away. Suspecting they'd been destroyed wasn't the same thing as learning they were actually gone. She wanted to cry out, instead, she squeezed her eyes shut.

Three more piles. I only needed to look through three more piles. She'd been so close to unraveling the mystery of those papers. How could her chance be destroyed? A tear crept from the corner of her eye and slid down her cheek. She'd followed a fork in the road, and clearly, she'd made the wrong choice. Now she had neither the wolf nor the papers.

"I need some fresh air. I'll be back," June said, the coverlet falling to her lap as she sat upright. She wanted to see the remains with her own eyes. Maybe there was something left.

"It's nearly dark. I'll go with you."

June held up her hand. "It's not dark yet, and I'd prefer that you didn't."

For once, Aza didn't assert her will. She just sat in the armchair and watched while June got up from the couch, put on her coat, and headed to the backyard.

Outside, red, orange, and yellow leaves hung from the trees. The countryside was quiet, and the smell of smoke filled the October air. A scent June normally associated with campfires and autumn, it now took on a dark characteristic as it burned the back of her throat. Drawing closer to the large hole, orange embers flickered amidst minute flecks of white paper. A pit opened in her own chest.

There was *nothing* left.

She balled her fists and lifted her eyes to the sky. She hadn't missed George this badly in a long time. Looking back down at the large black ditch, her gaze caught on the garage. The nearly forgotten building had been George's favorite place. Until today, entering this space had been unthinkable, the pain of proximity to so many things that were of him but not him was too much to bear. Overcome with longing for him, and desperate for answers, she walked there now.

June flipped on the fluorescent overhead light, glad that it still worked after years of disuse. Bracing herself for potential complaints from small animals who'd likely taken up residence in those years, she stepped inside and headed toward the back where he kept his workbench and tools. She breathed a sigh of relief when she reached the handmade bench, and only silence greeted her. It felt so good to be in his space. Why hadn't she come out here sooner? Everything was just as he left it: an assortment of tools, ladders, and his prized possession—the cherry red 1947 Chevy pickup. Hank used the snow blower and lawn mower when he took care of the yard, but other than that, nothing had been moved in four years.

Wrapping her arms around herself, June pretended they were George's. Closing her eyes, she imagined him there now, bent over his workbench, focused on some project. *"My beautiful bride, how did you know? I was just about to take a break?"* he'd ask with a smile as he pushed the project to the side. The man never treated her like an unwanted interruption. Always made her feel like her presence was a treat. Those marble eyes would twinkle as he stretched his arms wide for a hug.

Pained by an image that was no substitute for the real thing, June opened her eyes and stepped to the truck her husband had lovingly restored. Her fingers traced the chrome finishes and caressed the rich metallic paint, stopping to peer inside the pristine glass windshield. He'd explained the right glass, clear and unblemished, made all the difference in any car. As she squinted past all of her memories of Sunday drives in that car, a glint of something caught her eye in the truck's bed.

Racing to the rear, she seized a paper fragment. How did this get outside? That's when she remembered—George had been fastidious about recycling. After reading the papers, he'd stack the week's pile into neat little pancake-like bundles, tying them up with twine. Looping a little handle on the top, he carried them into the garage until the recycling truck came every other week. Or was it every month?

It didn't matter.

What mattered was that *those* were the papers he'd been obsessing over in the days leading up to his disappearance. There was a possibility George had left some here.

Fifteen minutes later, after frantically searching every corner and even the attic, June found herself frustrated and back at

George's workbench. The storage area there seemed too compact for papers. Not wanting to rule any space unexamined, June got on her tiptoes and swung open the cabinet doors above his workbench, empty but for a few rusted cans of paint and insecticide. A massive wave of disappointment closed around her. She slammed her fists on the countertop. Where could they be? A small drawer at the base of the cabinet sprung open, likely from the force.

Her brows raised. She'd totally missed this spot.

She knelt down. That was when she saw it—there, sitting in the far-left corner, under George's workbench. His last bundle of seven papers, neatly bound with twine. June closed the cabinet door, looking over her shoulder to make sure neither Aza nor Hank had followed her out to the garage. If they learned of this bundle, it would end up in the fire too. Seeing no one, June let out a long exhale, and her shoulders relaxed for the first time in four long years.

June smiled. *I'm going to find you, my love. I'm going to find you.*

***

Back in the house, June draped her coat over a chair in the kitchen, her footfalls echoing on the linoleum then wooden floor as she moved through the house to the living room. She needed to figure out a way to get Hank and Aza back on the road.

A dull glow radiated from the television screen, where credits rolled along to a happy instrumental. She rearranged the doily on the coffee table several times, the tips of her fingers twitching as she did. They would have betrayed her, but thankfully, Aza was deep under the spell of the television.

"*Whew!* That fresh air did wonders for my head. I don't know what came over me," June said, sinking back onto the couch. "The noise gave me such a start. I feel better now."

"It's the papers. See? I knew you'd feel better once we got them out of here. You really need to listen to me more often." Aza picked up the remote, flipping through the channels until she found an eighties comedy on one of the local network stations.

"Yes. Mmhmm. Hank isn't back yet, is he?"

"No." Aza crossed one slender leg over the other at the ankle. "You know, I did all that work and not even a thank you."

"Thank you." June hoped her tone didn't sound as forced as it felt.

"I don't think you mean it."

"You came into my home and moved my things without my permission and you really expect a thanks?"

"Do you have any idea how crazy you sound? I didn't 'move things.' I threw away four years of junk. I got rid of a fire hazard. And don't think I don't know why you were holding on to all that crap, either. Those crazy stacks of paper were your totems of *him*."

Each use of the word 'crazy' struck like a lash across June's soul. But she tried to ignore it because trying as her daughter was, June recognized the hurt of abandonment when she saw it. George hadn't just left her behind. He'd walked away from his entire family.

"Stop. Please. I don't want to go over this again." June rubbed her now throbbing temple.

"Yeah, well, I do. It's batshit *crazy*. He's gone and he's not coming back."

June merely nodded and pretended interest in the television. When Aza was in one of these moods, talking was futile.

"And now you're giving me the silent treatment?" Aza shook her head, but to June's relief, she didn't say anything more. A rarity, to be sure. It wasn't like her to give up so easily.

The next few hours stretched painfully. June waited for Hank to return and prayed he failed in his mission to hunt the wolf.

Finally, during a commercial break, Hank stormed into the kitchen, a blast of cold fall air trailing him. "He's a smart one. And huge too. Must have come all the way down from Canada." Hank stopped at the fridge and snagged a beer from the six-pack Aza left there for him. He popped the top and took a long guzzle. "I had him for a while, but he doubled back twice on his own trail. He knew I was following him. He was trying to shake me! Don't worry, smart guy like that won't be back tonight, Ms. June."

Oh, how she hoped he was wrong. There was an answer in that wolf. He didn't show up at her door with that thing in his mouth for no reason. June was sure of it. Since he'd appeared, her thoughts seemed to crystalize, too. No, he couldn't be gone for good.

Aza remained oddly silent in the face of Hank's assurances regarding the wolf. Now, she leaned forward in the armchair and planted both stockinged feet firmly on the ground before her, elbows on her knees. "Mom, this latest episode was too much. Hank and I have decided that it's time you come to stay with us. Why don't you pack a bag, and we can come later in the week for the rest?"

It wasn't a question, and now June understood her daughter's earlier silence. June patted Aza's hand. "You heard Hank, darling, the wolf won't be back. There's no need for me to go anywhere."

Aza shot Hank a look, and the big man's shoulders wilted a smidge. June could tell he regretted his bragging words. "Well, you never know. He *is* a smart one," Hank muttered.

"I doubt he's smart enough to open the door and let himself inside." June smiled.

"Mom, this is serious. If you don't come live with us, I think we're going to have to consider an alternative. And your granddaughter would never forgive me for that."

June's brows shot up, her emotions at war. Any mention of her granddaughter, Zala, warmed June's heart. A wild seed from the start, they'd always shared a special connection. Currently, Zala was off in Africa—according to the postcard June had received last week. But her daughter's words were nothing short of infuriating. "My independence is not for you to control," June said, struggling to keep her tone even.

"This isn't about control, Mom. It's about caring. About love. I don't want to see you hurt. That's why I'm prepared to petition for guardianship if you fight me on this. Between the papers and what we saw today, I have no doubt that a court would grant it to me. I already talked to a lawyer."

June gasped. "You wouldn't!"

"Not happily, but I don't think I have a choice."

June exhaled. Where had June and George gone wrong? How had they raised a daughter so different from either of them? "There's *always* a choice."

But June studied Aza. Her chin was set, her brows and full lips pulled into straight, no-nonsense lines. She had seen that look on her daughter's face before. Clearly, Aza had convinced herself there was no other way, that this was the only option.

June did a quick calculation of the probable outcomes, expelling a long, weary sigh as she reached her conclusion. Arguing was futile. Her age alone would present an uphill battle with most judges. The odds just weren't in her favor. She rubbed her forehead. It appeared as though *she* was the one who'd been left with no choice. Maybe tomorrow she'd come up with a work-around, but today, she just wanted both of them to leave. "Just give me a couple of weeks to say my goodbyes alone." In any negotiation, you had to start big and go small. Never worked in reverse.

"A week," Aza said.

June huffed and ran her hand across her forehead. As much as it galled her that she was having to bargain for her independence with her own child, some of this reaction was for show. Her mind had already kicked into strategy mode. If the papers could lead her to George, all of this would be moot. Her daughter would finally realize that June's faith wasn't some evidence of a mental defect, but a trait worthy of the utmost respect. June probably didn't need a week, but she *did* need her daughter and son-in-law out of her house. *Now*.

"I guess I'll have to make a week work. Starting tonight." June pursed her lips and gave the door a pointed look.

"That's fair," Aza said, readying to leave. Hank and Aza said their goodbyes shortly thereafter, and June nearly clapped. At least for now, she had her home back to herself.

Chafed as she was by their conversation, she didn't have one second to spare for resentment. Picking up the remote, June clicked off the television, and positioned herself to the side of the window, holding her breath until the truck's headlights disappeared down the road. When the last bit of light died, June stuffed her feet into a pair of old tennis shoes, snatched a flannel from the coat rack, and headed back out to the garage.

***

Ten minutes later, June sat on the edge of her couch, hunched over the bundle, skimming the dates at the top of each paper. She slid the most recent one out of the pile. If the papers had indeed triggered George's disappearance, surely the last one would hold the answer.

Dated October 30, 2016, this was the paper George had been reading the morning of his disappearance. Four years to the date exactly. Opening it, she reverently smoothed the edges with her hand. A spider scuttled out from between the pages. She let it scamper down the leg of the coffee table and under the couch. June perched her reading glasses on her nose. "Okay, George, what did you see?"

The front page held stories about a city council decision on water reclamation and a feature about a recent fire. Built in 1845, the house once belonging to Marcus Bollingreen had burned to the ground. For years, it'd served as a stop on the Underground Railroad. The paper had a picture of the house that must have been taken fifty years ago, judging from the cars on the street in front of it. According to the caption, that was the day it received historic landmark status for its anti-slavery legacy.

June remembered the house and the metal sign posted in the yard out front. The house next door had a Confederate flag hanging from its porch. But that wasn't why it stood out. The Bollingreen house had once belonged to George's family. For years, his brother lived there. Was it possible the fire had prompted George's disappearance?

June frowned, trying to remember what became of that brother. Leon? She'd only met him a few times. A quiet one, but polite. When he came to visit, he never stayed long and the brothers always spent their time in the woods out back—"hunting," George would say. Eventually, Leon sold the house to some folks from up near the Michigan border. That was a good thirty years ago, too long for there to be a connection. Besides, according to the article, the fire harmed no one. June didn't see why that would be cause for a happily married man to walk out on his life.

They had found a Native woman dead in her barn. Foul play was suspected. June peered at the small black and white memorial photo. Neither the name nor the picture from her memorial looked familiar. But, stranger or no, her heart ached for the woman. No one had the right to take another's life.

June turned the page.

A small headline leaped out at her. In the lower-left corner, tucked between a car dealership's ad and the crease of the next page, it read: *Wolf Sighting Near Kimball Factory.*

June leaned forward, drawn close by the words themselves. This was no coincidence. As her intuition had told her earlier—*that wolf has answers.*

Around midnight, she turned out the light near the front window. She wasn't tired then, but knew she would be the next day if she didn't sleep soon.

Aza had left a cup of milky tea and a cheese sandwich on a plate in case June got hungry. June carried the tea and plate into the kitchen. She covered the sandwich with plastic wrap and put it in the fridge for lunch tomorrow. Emptying the lukewarm tea into the sink, streaks of white in the light brown liquid reminded her of the horror that had greeted her that morning. Scared to look down, she pulled her blouse away from her chest anyway.

June sighed in relief. The fabric was still dry. Maybe she'd imagined it? No. She hadn't. Something strange was going on. As she stood before the sink, a shadow in the yard caught her attention.

She moved closer to the kitchen window, peering into the darkness. The rain hadn't returned all day and the Milky Way shone clear again. Millions of stars illuminated his long silhouette, turning the brown to gray and dark blue in the strange light. His golden eyes, shining like two large, yellow diamonds, stared directly into hers.

The small hairs on June's forearms stood. She wanted to step outside, but the conversation with Aza held her back.

The wolf inclined his head and turned, the shadows swallowing him in seconds. And as she stared into the darkness, panic crept into her chest. She couldn't help but wonder if standing still was a mistake. No. It was too late. She would follow him tomorrow.

SEVEN

Present

A wolf. A fire. And a murdered Native woman. Did they have anything to do with each other? More importantly to June, did they have anything to do with her husband's disappearance?

These questions rolled through her mind the next morning, as she stood in front of the cellar shelves, arms folded, eyes squinting, taking everything in. Before he'd disappeared, this had been George's other domain. One that she'd happily ceded, repelled by the suffocatingly low ceiling and shadows rife with the dank smell of mold. The odor was especially strong now with all the recent rain. She hadn't been down here in years, but the spiders sure had. A curtain of thick cobwebs hung on the top row and in all the corners of every shelf.

June found an old broom and whisked away the webs, simultaneously unsettling a thick coating of dust that made her nose twitch. She waved it away. Now that the space was clear, she saw the shelves contained clear bags of Christmas decorations, but also several crates and unmarked boxes. June yanked the first crate down, bracing herself for spiders as she pulled off the burlap cloth covering.

Bottles, not spiders, were all she found. Breathing a sigh of relief, she eased one out of the crate. Her mouth puckered as the question—*what is this?*—almost crossed her lips. Remembering she was alone in the basement, she let the words die unspoken. Based on the shape, they were wine bottles. Most of the labels were peeling and faded. She shuffled through them, stopping at a bottle in the middle of the case.

The year on the label was 1865. Had to be a misprint. June slid it back into the case and pulled out another. The year on this label was 1842. June set it on the cement floor next to the crate and plucked out a third bottle: 1834.

Shee sat on the cold, hard floor. Where had George come across these gems? The labels were too faded for her to make out any but the last three letters of one bottle: *U-S-E*. More than likely the name of the estate where they'd been filled.

Rolling the bottle back and forth in her hand, her gaze drifted to the shelf. The first day she spoke to George, he'd been stacking bottles at her father's five and dime, sitting on the floor, something like she was now. So many years ago. Time had dulled neither her crisp recollection of that afternoon nor the passion she felt for the man—*her* man.

She set aside the bottles. No doubt they were worth a pretty penny. At some point, she may have to look into their origins, but until she could find someone who specialized in possibly antique wines, they were of no help to her now.

Standing, she pulled down the next box. It contained a random mess of bolts and screws of various sizes. Odd, given her husband's penchant for neatness. She let the box drop to the floor. As she did, it tipped on its side, spilling the contents. *Damn, just what I need!* June kneeled, righting the crate. She scooped a handful of metal, then paused, squinting to better see the bottom of the crate.

What is that? A latch?

June set the bolts back on the floor and tucked her finger under a small loop protruding from the inside of the box. Tugging, the metal sheet lifted on the second yank. *A false bottom?* She peeled it back, finagling the sides stuck to the edges after years of immobility and rust.

Underneath, lay a perfectly preserved daguerreotype from the 1850s. She recognized it at once because the old style of photograph had been popular with her adoptive grandparents. It'd been ages since she'd seen one.

But what exactly was she looking at? People, for sure—but without her reading glasses, and in the dim cellar light, their faces were blurry. Making them out felt like an eye exam she was failing. Sure this treasure hadn't been secreted away for nothing, June tucked two of the bottles under her arm and carried the picture upstairs.

Sunlight poured into the living room window. She glanced out of it, half expecting to see the wolf, but he hadn't come today. She grabbed her reading glasses from the coffee table and held the picture to the light. Her jaw dropped.

It was an image of the Bay Harbor Lighthouse on Lake Eerie. She'd always loved the old stone towers that guided fishermen to safety and remembered reading about this one in history class as a girl. Standing in front of the keeper's door were twelve men, two rows of six, who appeared to be in their twenties, wearing black suits and thin ties. In the center of the front row stood her George. Not a family member bearing a strong resemblance, but her very own husband. She'd know his face anywhere. Though, the last place she expected to see it was in a picture from the 1850s.

She also recognized several of the other faces: Jack, Samuel, Keith, and George's two other brothers, Ambrose and Conrad. In the background, hills sloped up for acres. Dotting them were rows and rows of grapevines. June picked the bottle back up, squinting at the label. Six lines, four at 45-degree angles—the faint outline of a lighthouse.

June looked out the window at the cornfields across the empty road as disbelief washed over her. How could this be?

The lighthouse had burned down in the storm of 1873. Lightning struck it, and, even in the heavy rain, the entire building went up in flames, leaving behind nothing but cinders. How was it possible that her husband, only two years older than her, stood before a lighthouse destroyed almost fifty years before he was born?

Had he stumbled on a portal to a parallel universe? Traveled through time? Or was it some sort of Faustian bargain?

Maybe her identification was wrong, and the last letters on the bottle were just a coincidence. June went to the kitchen and returned with a magnifying glass. She held it to the photo, examining the intricate details. There, in the corner of the vineyard, was a sign. Bay Harbor Lighthouse.

She clutched the magnifying glass as her heart hammered and her mind raced to come up with a logical explanation. This all but confirmed her initial thoughts. Her George had walked the earth almost 150 years ago. Her mind spun. The implications were staggering; the love of her life, the man she thought she knew better than anyone else in the world, was capable of...magic.

What other secrets had he concealed?

The phone ringing in the kitchen interrupted June's racing thoughts. Normally, she didn't answer when it rang. Most of the time, a telemarketer was on the other end, having come up with some new spiel trying to separate her from her money.

"Hello?" she finally said on the fourth ring, having made her way to the kitchen, driven by a sudden desperate need for contact with the outside world.

"Hi, Mom. Do you want some help going through things?" Aza's voice was softer than usual, her form of an apology. "I realize this is a lot for one person, especially in such a short time. I should have offered yesterday."

June didn't need help going through boxes, but she did with sorting through her new discovery. Most of her friends had died long ago. Her daughter was just about the only voice of relative reason she had to talk to.

But if she told her daughter she thought George was a time traveler trapped in a distant year, the end result would likely be an expedited removal from the house. Aza would find some way to discount the photo. Or maybe it would be enough?

June hesitated, her words caught in her throat, her mind wrestling with the enormity of her discovery. She opened and closed her mouth in search of the right words and absently twirled the phone cord with her fingers to relieve her mounting anxiety.

There was no way to pull that off, not with their complicated history. A crushing sense of isolation struck her. Yet another weight she would have to bear alone. She summoned a fragile smile. "I'm fine, sweetie. It's nice of you to offer. Things are coming along well. I was just down in the basement looking through some boxes."

"The basement?" Worry sent her daughter's pitch up two octaves. "Mom, you shouldn't be going up and down the stairs like that."

June sighed, definitely glad she hadn't mentioned the time traveling. "I go up and down the stairs to bed every night, as I have been doing for a very, very long time." Honestly, she wondered what gave Aza the impression she was physically frail.

"I see your sarcasm is still intact."

June laughed. "Glad you've still got enough humor to recognize it."

"It's hard to miss." Aza paused. "On the topic of ill humor, I have some news you won't like."

June braced herself. "Go ahead."

"They caught the wolf."

June took a moment to respond, her insides churning. She didn't want to know. But she had to ask. "Caught?"

"Dusty Bore shot it out in the woods behind Leed's farm. So you won't have to worry about it coming around bothering you anymore."

Pain clenched June's chest. *The wolf is dead?* Poor thing.

"Mom, are you still there?"

"I'm still here." June's eyes moistened. She leaned against the kitchen wall. The air suddenly gone from her lungs, she slid down the wall, sitting on the floor.

"You sound upset. I hope you're not upset about the wolf. Wolves are dangerous killers. We don't need them in our community. There are children a few miles from that area."

"*Dangerous*. Sometimes I think that label is overused." June rubbed her forehead.

"You've always been such a softy when it comes to animals, Mom. It's not normal to think they're on the same level as humans. What's normal is for humans to exterminate those that present a threat."

June had dragged herself to the telephone thinking that the reality of the call might ground her, but it only made her want to flee.

"Mom? Are you still there?"

"Yes, and I heard you. A threat." That wolf didn't strike her as threatening. But even if it was, her neighbors' *shoot first, question later* approach to life sickened her. June also had the feeling that the wolf had come to her for a reason, and now, she would never know. Oh, dear... Why hadn't she followed him? She shook her head, pushing a breath through the heaviness in her chest. She still had the picture, and that felt like something. Right now, it would have to be enough.

"Mom, I don't like killing animals either, okay? But if it comes down to human or wolf, you know what my choice is. Anyway, there's nothing we can do about it now. It's done. And I have good news too. Your granddaughter is on the way back to the States. I told her you wouldn't want any help, but Zala wouldn't take no for an answer."

June paused. Her daughter's move from one topic to the next gave June emotional whiplash. Especially today. Though she was right, the mere mention of Zala raised her spirits. "I thought she was in Africa?"

"She was. Rather, she is. But she won't be for much longer. She said she had a feeling you needed her."

"I hope you didn't put that idea in her head!"

Aza scoffed. "As if she'd ever listen to me. Anyway, if you don't want my help, I'm going to get started on Hank's laundry."

Despite her tremendous upset, after saying their goodbyes, June hung up the phone with a reluctant but genuine smile. Zala was coming.

If there was one person in the world she could confide in, it was her granddaughter. It would be so good to see her, even though she felt bad she had cut her trip short. But June wasn't at all surprised. There'd always been something fiercely loyal and protective about Zala. No doubt she picked up that trait from her grandfather.

EIGHT

1949

Jeffrey took longer to recover from the attack than June. His mother said it was the concussion. June suspected it was something else, fear possibly, but her own reasons kept her from questioning too deeply. As long as Jeffrey was leery of coming outside, George continued to walk her to the store.

June could tell George was upset about the fact that she'd been attacked. He'd taken it as a personal failing, and even while they were at the store, she caught him watching her protectively whenever the door opened.

He hadn't mentioned their connection again and she appreciated that, but it was still there. This huge, unspoken mass of emotion hovered over them regardless of whether they were together or apart. It came across in subtle smiles and the way he never let her walk on the outside of the sidewalk. He knew she liked strawberries, which were so expensive her father didn't even stock them in his store—yet, somehow, George managed to show up on her doorstep with a basket of ripe, juicy ones several times a week.

"After you," George said one afternoon as he held the door of her father's store open for her. June's shoulder brushed his chest as she slid inside. She hadn't realized how close he was and the touch, even through her jacket, heated her skin.

Pleasantly startled, June shrugged off her coat and slipped it onto the rack next to the door. Out of the corner of her eye, she glimpsed George's jaw tightening. Curious, but also eager to say hello to her father, June didn't inquire.

"Ah, there you are, my sweet girl," her father said, holding his arm wide for a side hug. "How's your mama?"

"Hi, Dad. She's resting comfortably." June gave him a peck on the cheek.

"Good. Good. Everything's been humming along here too." Turning to George, her father's smile broadened. "Thank you, son, for seeing to my daughter."

George nodded. June tilted her head in surprise. "Son" was the term her father normally reserved for Jeffrey. He wasn't the type to throw around endearments. Clearly, George had made an impression.

June helped her father into his coat as he casually questioned her, trying to ascertain whether the walk over had been too jarring. In the last several days, this was a daily occurrence. Hand on the doorknob, he turned to her, whispering in her ear, "You'll tell me if something is bothering you?"

"I promise, Daddy. I will."

Her father ran his hand over her hair. "Okay, Pumpkin. I'll see you at dinner." Satisfied, he slipped outside to go see about his wife.

The door wasn't closed one minute before George walked over to her. "Did *he* do that to you?" His lips twitched, and June could tell he was trying to control his emotions.

Embarrassed, she looked down at her arm, pulling on the sleeve even though the cat was already out of the bag. June had worn long-sleeved dresses every day since her encounter with Jeffrey to conceal her bruising, but the sleeve must have ridden up when she took off her coat.

"Which *he*?" June said, stalling for time as she looked back up at George. It wasn't that she wanted to protect Jeffrey. She was just confused. The marks were barely visible. How had George even noticed them?

But notice them, he had.

"Those prints are too small for the man who attacked you, so we both know which 'he' I'm talking about. Are you trying to take up for him?" Now, the anger radiated off of George in thick waves. It was so potent it almost knocked her over, so palpable it stuck to her skin. She should have been afraid. Instead, seeing the concern beneath, it acted on her like the most intense aphrodisiac known to man, unleashing a torrent of desire that had her eyes darting to the storeroom. Where these intense feelings could lead scared her; her knowledge of happenings between men and women didn't go far beyond a few stolen kisses on the walk home. Whereas before, she'd been content to wait for marriage, suddenly, she wanted to know everything and she wanted George to be her teacher.

Jeffrey had never made her feel like this. She doubted any man on earth except George ever could.

The realization was delicious, but the swiftness also made June slightly woozy. Almost like there was some mystical undercurrent to their attraction.

"Answer me," George said, his voice lower now, breathy, almost like he sensed where her mind had gone and it had left him reeling too. "Why are you protecting him?"

"I'm not trying to protect anyone. But how do you know anything about the size of the man who attacked me?" June paused, her heartbeat accelerating, her mind clearing. "Since last week, you are the only person who hasn't asked me anything about that man. Like what he looked like, or if I'd ever seen him before. I understand giving space, but something tells me that isn't why you haven't brought it up. You all but warned me he was on his way that day. I think you knew it was going to happen?" She'd said it like a question, but there was no doubt in her mind. He knew, but how and why was a mystery.

"Did that coward do that to you?" George's tone was firm.

"If I say yes, what will you do?" June spat out, exasperated.

George shook his head. "Marry me."

June made a sound that was part laugh, part gasp, all astonishment. Was he toying with her? Now? She crossed her arms. "Shock and misdirection? Clever trick, but it's not going to work on me."

He pressed those beautiful lips together and leaned so close her world swayed. His eyes narrowed and it looked like he had something to say, but he wasn't sure if he should. "You and I, we're like pieces of a puzzle, cut by fate itself. I was built to protect you. As your husband, I'll be able to keep away the likes of Jeffrey and any other beast who dares to come near you."

June nodded. Once. Not out of comprehension, but in order to give her brain a physical kick-start. He'd said a mouthful and her head was swimming with a million different thoughts and questions. "Beast? Jeffrey may not be the man for me but I wouldn't quite call him a beast."

That wasn't exactly where she'd meant to land in terms of first thoughts out of her mouth, but she was glad she had. Nothing could have been sexier than the glint that sparkled in George's eye at June's admission that Jeffrey was not the one for her. For an instant, she was tempted to stop talking, but he still hadn't answered her question and she had to know. The timing of everything was just too strange. The day George started working for her father, she was attacked by a madman. What if they were connected? What if George wasn't the man she thought he was? What if the man she'd been dreaming of day and night wanted to cause her harm?

"I need you to answer me. Did you know it was going to happen, George?"

"I didn't know, but I had a sense that danger was closing." The anger returned, making his oddly colored eyes gleam bright blue and green.

"A sense? About me?"

He nodded.

"How?"

He shrugged. "Let's just say I have a nose for danger. Call it animal instinct."

June eyed him. "Animal instinct? That's a strange thing to say, George Chambray." She wiped a finger across her lips, debating whether to ask the question on the tip of her tongue. "You talk about animal instinct, and I want to understand. Were you in the war?"

Normally, she wouldn't have been so forward, but he'd just proposed, if you could say that about his declaration, and almost all of her had wanted to say yes. If he waited a week and asked again, she was pretty sure she *would* say yes. But there were a few things she wanted to know before she did. Like where he'd come from before he showed up in her life.

"I was. My five brothers and I all went off to war."

A vision of him and his brothers in peril clouded her mind with sadness. "Did they…?" She couldn't finish the question. She wasn't sure if it was even appropriate to ask.

"Make it back? Yes."

"Were they…?"

"Hurt? Everyone came out whole, but not necessarily intact. War takes its toll." He clenched his fist. There wasn't a knuckle on either hand devoid of thick scars. His jaw tightened, and his eyes brimmed with sadness. She wanted to stamp out his sorrow, fill his eyes and his days with soothing warmth. June vowed never to bring up the topic again unless he did. It didn't matter what brought him to her side, just that he was there.

She ran her fingertips in small circles over his knuckles, lightly; the touch awakening something powerful in each of them. For a moment, it felt as if time stopped.

Dizzy with desire, June smiled shyly. George unclenched his fist, opening his calloused palm and taking her fingers. The tips sizzled under his touch. Eyes sparkling, he lifted her hand and brushed his lips against her skin, leaving one puckered kiss that felt like a million blazing strokes along her breasts and deep in her core.

"*Yes.*"

"Yes?" George asked, his eyes round with laughter and love. "As in, yes, you will be Mrs. George Chambray?"

June lifted her chin to nod, but before she could finish the motion, George pressed his lips against her mouth in a kiss at once so sweet, so tender, and so passionate, she knew he'd spoken the truth when he said that he was made for her—and she for him.

That evening, George asked June's father for his daughter's hand in marriage. Her parents were shocked, but even they could see the rightness of June and George. They married one week later.

Their honeymoon lasted sixty-eight years. True to his word, he taught her how to protect herself. He also taught her how to live off the land and be a farmer's wife. The only thing he didn't teach her how to do was to go on without him. It was one thing she would forever refuse to learn.

Nine

Present

The rain had returned. A steady drizzle, cold and wet. Typical for fall in Ohio. Come October, most people figured it'd be a good seven months before the sun came back around and started to make a steady appearance.

June wouldn't let something as small as the weather stand in her way. She threw on a coat and a pair of rain boots, slamming the door behind her. In two days, she hadn't been able to make much sense of the clues she'd uncovered. But she knew someone who might have a sensible explanation for why she'd found what appeared to be a young photo of George from the 1850s.

Three hours later, June put George's old Chevy in park, hopped out of the car, and walked over to a wooden gate with a huge *Road Closed* sign nailed to it. She lifted the plank and drove through.

The road was overgrown and narrow, with ferns creeping over the edges and cracks wide enough to swallow a smaller car. Several times, June had to swerve onto the shoulder to avoid rutting her tires. She passed the skeleton of a long-abandoned barn and the stone façade of an old mill. The road forked at a weathered clapboard church. One direction went nowhere, forks upon forks upon forks. The other dead ended at the cemetery where George's tombstone stood.

Apart from George's, no new tombstones had been placed there in decades. The town emptied when the government forced the residents to evacuate on account of a chemical spill.

June parked on the road at the edge of the cemetery, which was surrounded by a knee-high iron fence covered in ivy. Clearing the gate with no effort, she made her way to the back of the plot near the mausoleum.

The ground around George's headstone was damp, covered with leaves and long grass. June didn't bother to maintain the site because the grave was empty—as she hoped it would remain until long after she was gone. She barely gave it a second glance as she stepped over and walked to the edge of the cemetery, damp leaves and mud making a sucking sound as she did.

She'd allowed the tombstone to be cut and placed for her family's benefit. To give them closure. They picked this place because George loved it. "The lore," he had said, "keeps the space protected." Locals had long believed the town was haunted by those killed in the chemical spills.

The lore wasn't the only thing that protected the area. Once a year, in October, Samuel came to the old ghost town and reposted signs warning travelers to keep out. He made new paths that misdirected those who didn't heed the signs. June knew this because, for sixty-plus years, she and George would join him.

Occasionally, George's other brothers would meet there as well. It was a strange ritual. As far as June knew, they did it out of observance for their own lost family, of whom none of them ever spoke. Tending the area as they did, June affectionately referred to them as the "ghost crew."

After George's disappearance, June had been too consumed with shock to make the annual trek. The second year, she had missed Samuel when she did come. Last year, he had sent her away, refusing to speak with her.

Well, she wasn't leaving this year. She patted the pocket of her coat. Not without answers.

"Samuel!" June called. Her voice echoed in the forest. A flock of ravens took flight from the treetops, their wings clapping noisily as they sped away.

June turned in a circle, searching the dense trees. The woods hummed with the life that reclaimed them in the absence of human intervention. Abundant plant and animal life. But she didn't hear the stirrings of man, other than her own breath—small white puffs in the chill autumn air. "I know you're there, Samuel." And though she couldn't see him, with the same surety she knew her husband lived, she knew Samuel was there. Watching.

"I can feel your eyes, Samuel!" June leaned down and picked up a stick, whittling the ends with her fingers to keep her hands busy as she waited. "I'll be here for as long as it takes!"

"You shouldn't have come." Samuel's voice was cold and harsh, almost menacing. It came from behind her somewhere.

"I'm here, and I'm not leaving until you tell me where my husband is! You don't want to find out what I'm willing to do to get an answer!"

The tall, slightly bow-legged man stepped out of the woods to June's right. He was wearing his earth-colored hunting cape and heavy black boots. The hood pulled over his head cast much of his face in shadow.

"Your husband is dead, woman. You'd do best to get that through your thick skull and stop all of this foolish talk before someone has you committed."

June's temper flared. Nine times out of ten, in her experience, when a man called a woman "crazy," it was because she saw something he didn't want her to see or said something he wasn't willing to hear. Anecdotal experience notwithstanding, June was positive there was nothing wrong with her mind and resented the implication. It was the same thing he'd said last year. The only difference—and really there was only *one* because, like her and her husband, the man didn't age noticeably—was what she'd found in the box.

"He's *not* dead! I know it, and so do you!" June pulled the daguerreotype showing her husband with Samuel and the other men from the inside of her coat.

Samuel's thick, wild eyebrows shot up, momentarily disappearing into the shadows of his hood. As quickly as they'd risen, he adjusted his expression. "Is this supposed to mean something to me, woman?"

June adjusted her stance, pissed and ready to square off against the cantankerous old man. "Keep your 'woman' shit and just tell me what the hell you know. I've seen the wolf too!" A sharp twinge of sadness gripped her as she mentioned the animal that had been hunted down recently.

Samuel took a step back, as if he'd been struck. He was silent for a long while. "I'm not going to entertain this." But his voice had shifted from cold and harsh to... scared? It was almost imperceptible. Anyone else probably wouldn't have noticed, but June Chambray wasn't *anyone else*. This man had answers about her husband, and she was keyed into him so deeply she could see the vein on the left side of his neck cording as he tried to calm himself.

Is it the picture or seeing the wolf that has him this shaken? she wondered.

"Save your gaslighting for the next person, Samuel! That wolf means something. Why are you so afraid to tell me?"

"There are no wild wolves in Ohio. You need to get back in your truck and leave."

June narrowed her eyes. "How do you explain this picture? Do you think George would want you to keep this from me? You disloyal son of a bitch! Is this how you repay your brother's fidelity?"

"How dare you question my loyalty, you ignorant woman! Have you ever thought that your husband left for a reason? That he doesn't want to be found?"

"I don't know what kind of bad luck love story you've experienced, but there's no doubt in my mind that George wants me there, wherever he is. Is that why you're being so tightlipped? You can't stand to see two people happy?"

Enraged, Samuel whirled on his heels and sped back into the forest. Smiling, June gave chase.

That was the thing about hotheads. You could always goad them into reacting thoughtlessly. If she could follow him back to the place he'd come from, maybe she'd be able to find more clues about his connection with George.

The man was fast, and though she was unnaturally quick for her age, she'd underestimated how well he knew the area. He dipped into a grove of trees and disappeared.

June rocked back on her heels, a bittersweet satisfaction lifting her heart. He'd all but admitted that George was still alive. But he was gone now, and June knew he wouldn't come back again, no matter how many times she called or how long she waited. He'd gone, and he took the most important information with him—George's whereabouts.

June walked back to the tombstone bearing George's name. Studying it now, she saw a mound of dirt about the size of a bowling ball—freshly piled. Covering it were large paw prints...
The wolf?

Had the prints and mound been here when she arrived?

June scanned the cemetery. The steady hush of wind whispered through late-stage autumn leaves. Her eyes and ears told her she was alone.

She dropped to her knees and began clawing at the moist soil. Thankfully, it was recently dug because the ground was already hardening in preparation for winter. In seconds, she'd unearthed a hunk of metal. Flecks of red dirt clung to it. Wiping the dirt on her pants, she recognized the pendant at once, gold braided into a circle with raised etchings in the center that mirrored each other on either side.

This amulet belonged to George. How many times had she fingered it as it lay flat against his chest in bed? She knew the designs with her eyes closed. George was never without this necklace. The same necklace that had been in the wolf's mouth just days before.

Tears sprang to her eyes and she clutched the necklace to her lips. George's necklace. Hot tears rolled down her cheeks. Her mind raced with a million thoughts and emotions.

There must have been two wolves. Her wolf was still alive, and he'd been here recently. He knew she'd come. Knew she'd find this. But how could a wolf possess that level of intelligence?

June frowned. She'd come here for answers, and while she'd found some, they'd come at a cost—more questions. But now that she knew George was alive, nothing would keep her from finding him.

TEN

Later that night, a shrill Arctic wind whistled through a crack in the lower left corner of June's bedroom window frame. Around three a.m., it finally dragged her from bed. Her throat felt raw, probably from inhaling so much cold air, so she headed downstairs for a drink.

In the kitchen cabinet, twenty-four glasses, totems of her domestic life, sat pertly in three neat clusters. June took down a large one. It fit perfectly in her hand. She turned on the faucet, and a stream of cool water rushed out, bubbling up to the top and spilling over the sides. Standing there in the dark, leaning against the kitchen sink, she sipped, trying to recapture the bits and pieces of the strange dream eluding her like slippery fish.

The linoleum warmed beneath her bare, flat feet. Outside, the bitter wind whipped against the house, battering the shutters. June emptied and refilled her glass twice.

At last, the ball of fire in her throat disappeared. So, too, she acknowledged with some frustration, did the dream. There'd been an animal. Of that much, she was sure. And it'd felt desperate and lost. June leaned to place the glass in the sink.

Movement in the yard caught her attention. She froze, glass in mid-air.

The familiar yellow diamonds, eyes, *his* eyes, were looking directly at her.

He did not turn away this time. He merely lifted his head and howled. It was a long and mournful cry. Piercing and powerful, echoing off everything in the valley, including the stars. June held her breath, listening. It felt like someone had scooped out her insides, leaving a huge, cavernous space which she hoped might finally be filled.

At that moment, June remembered her dream: *a whale in a water glass*. The animal, brittle from thirst, stretched to catch a single drop of tea from a dollhouse cup perched on the lip of the water glass. June looked down at the glass in her own hand.

"A whale needs an ocean," she whispered.

June dropped the glass, indifferent to the sound of shards breaking.

Then, June Chambray walked out the back door, into the dead of night, and crossed the yard to the wolf. When she'd almost closed the distance between them, he rose, turned, and headed toward the Enchanted Forest. The treeline pulsed in the strong winds, as though it were a living thing, but this did not scare her because she knew this path would lead to George.

Several times, the wolf paused while June stopped to catch her breath. He guided her through a thicket of trees and over a small hill. She knew the area well.

The wolf stopped near the deep tarn where deer often came to drink—Dargin Lake, her daughter had named it. They walked around the large body of water then far beyond, finally stopping at a round cluster of bushes, dense and tall like a wall of trees, with a narrow opening in the middle.

The wolf waited, as though bidding June to enter. Curiosity outweighing her trepidation, she did, dropping to all fours in order to do so, brambles scraping at her skin as she crept forward. After what seemed like forever, the bushes ended in a hidden grotto dug into the side of the foothill.

There, in the center, two pups blindly moved about pawing one another. June drew nearer. The moisture had returned to her chest. Whereas before she'd felt the liquid bloom like a solitary rose on each breast, June now felt a bouquet blossoming.

One by one, the pups' noses sniffed the air. They must have picked up on her scent. They tumbled over one another, running toward her and licking at the small droplets of blood erupting on her arms and neck, instinctively trying to sooth her wounds with their small sandpaper tongues. The wolf sat on his haunches at the mouth of the cave. His stance shielded the grotto, like he'd been charged with protecting precious goods.

Utterly devoid of fear, June looked from him to the pups—understanding, at last.

Normally, June was never more present than in her dreams. Now, however, she saw every detail of this waking day, each blade of grass crossed to get here. She felt them bend beneath the weight of the raindrops which fell singularly and in slow motion. Mostly, she felt the wolf waiting patiently for her to decide.

June lay down on the dirt floor of the small rock cavern. In the tiny patch of sky still visible through the mouth of the cave, she saw a million stars and knew all of their names...like family. She opened up her robe, and her soft brown breasts flopped down across her chest. Scenting milk, the pups mouthed their way to her nipples, latched on, and suckled.

Each tug and pinch of the cubs' sharp teeth drew something more than milk from June. One by one, the barriers standing between her and a new understanding disintegrated, nudging her toward clarity. Her senses swirled with chaotic fury.

The pinching on June's nipples increased in intensity, growing from tolerable and restricted to her breasts, to searing and spreading up into her shoulders, down her arms, and into her fingertips. As it shot into her spine, the agony became greater and greater—like a supernova flaring, encompassing her entire body. She struggled out of her robe, suddenly too hot to endure the fabric. It felt like her skin was being stretched to its limit, then splitting and ripping from her muscle and bones, bones that were crumbling and reshaping themselves with an eerie fluidity.

But she knew that, no matter how severe, she wouldn't pull away from the babes; because this wasn't a supernova flaring through her, but the essence of motherhood—a living, breathing force that had chosen to occupy her. And through their fusing, it had gifted June with the ability to nurture life that did not come from her own womb.

"Where is their birth mother?" June asked the wolf when the excruciating pain had died down enough to speak.

"I don't really know. I found them like this. Alone and abandoned."

No doubt she was the wolf killed near Leeds the other day, June thought sadly.

"Poor pups." Only then did another crumbling barrier allow June to realize the impossible strangeness of speaking with a wolf. Her eyes snapped from the pups to the wolf. "How did you...? How is this happening? You speak English?"

The wolf laughed.

"I mean, you *speak*?" Two truths struck her simultaneously with such force that she temporarily fell out of time and place.

June was talking to a wolf. Because—*she* was a wolf.

The pups had stopped feeding but were asleep, grunting contentedly, while latched to two of her four nipples, their small bodies warm on her furry belly.

Fur. *Fur?*

A grey and white pelt covered her skin. June's eyes combed her form, slowed as much by shock as by the overwhelm of what she saw. She lifted her hand, only to realize paws had replaced her extremities. She no longer had to close one eye and look down to see her own nose. A snout—her snout—was clearly visible; in fact, it was so obtrusive that focusing on anything else was difficult. No, that wasn't what was making focusing difficult. Nor was it the fact that her tail was wagging so hard that her haunches were shaking.

I...am a wolf?

A scream rose inside of her that could split the world in two. But it didn't cross her lips—nay, muzzle. The cubs looked so peaceful as they slept. She couldn't bear the thought of disturbing them, especially after the tremendous loss they'd suffered.

"What's happening? What's going on?" She looked searchingly at the wolf.

The wolf cocked his head, inched his paws toward her in a way that brought his body lower to the ground. He crept closer. The movement instantly calmed June. Something in her understood him as well as if he'd spoken. He intended to reassure, to comfort.

"June, I know you have many questions, and I will try to answer them as best I can, but before I do, please, you must tell me, what did you do with the amulet that I left for you?"

"George's amulet?" June asked, utterly confused.

"Yes."

"Who are you, and what do you want with George's amulet?" She could see no possible connection between what must be an odd dream and the necklace George had worn every day of their life together. And if there was a connection, she hardly saw a reason to open up to this creature.

"I'm a friend, June. Someone you can trust, and if you just take a minute to breathe, you'll be able to feel that. What I'm saying is the truth."

"I don't know how I grew a tail, so forgive me if nothing is making enough sense right now for me to believe you."

Suddenly, the creature's face contorted. His snout contracted, reshaping into a human nose. The pelt of hair covering his body went smooth until...before her sat a naked man!

June's ears twitched as she stared at someone who looked just like one of George's younger brothers. *"Jack?* Is that you?"

"It's me." He shifted to conceal himself. "I am no stranger, and before I explain, I need you to tell me about the amulet."

"It's home. It's safe," June stammered.

Jack sighed, a long, deep sigh of relief. "Thank God. Then we have a chance."

"A chance? A chance at what? Jack, tell me— is George alive?"

Jack nodded. "He is." And as soon as the words left his mouth, he shifted again, his skin stretching, and this time, June noticed the surrounding air seemed to pulsate with colors she'd never seen before. But the colors disappeared almost as quickly as the realization dawned, allowing her confused mind to dance to the next glorious thought.

"He's alive? My George is alive?" Her tail wagged again. She knew it! For four long years, she'd known. She'd been doubted and derided, ridiculed by her own daughter, but she was right. The rush of hope that surged within her was so tremendous, for a moment, her concern for her own state evaporated. "Take me to him! Now! I beg you."

Jack shook his head, slowly, and June's chest tightened at the sadness in his eyes. "I don't know exactly where he is, but with your help, I hope to find him."

"*My* help? How can I help? Especially now?" She looked down at her body again. *Really* looked. This time, accepting that the body she was looking at was truly her own. A flood of panic swelled up inside of her so large it was suffocating. "What's happening to me? How is this possible?"

Jack inclined his head, his eyes holding a mixture of pride and solemnity. "You've made your first change. You're what's known by some as 'Dargin.' A child of ancient African ghost people who bred with humans millennia ago. Ours are able to change into wolf form."

Stunned, June blinked several times. *Dargin*? June listened as Jack told her about a magical people who'd gradually reduced in number and now lived in warring packs throughout the world. Though fascinating, throughout his story, one question nagged her.

"Dargin? That's the name my daughter gave to the water we passed on the way here," she said. "How did she know this word? Did one of you tell her about our history?"

Jack's eyes rounded, and she could scent his surprise. "No. We were all sworn to secrecy. No one would have told her. It's possible she just *knew*."

June thought about Aza, always blocking things out. Was that why? Like her, Aza had sensed she was different? Was her ultra-controlling nature a reaction to fear of her own uniqueness?

"So my daughter and granddaughter... are like us?"

"Probably, though it has been known to skip generations."

"Why? Why haven't any of us changed before?"

The wolf circled to the mouth of the cave and looked up at the moon. "I don't know for sure. Could be because you didn't know you could. Sometimes Dargin are raised in an environment ignorant of their nature and they manage to change. Some trigger, some emotional surge can be great enough to take you unawares and shift you. But that's rare. Usually, we only achieve what we're told we're capable of. Our kind do not differ from humans in that regard."

June looked down at the wolf pups and thought about her own daughter and granddaughter. Beyond naming the lake, Aza didn't seem to have any wolf in her. That made June sad. But Zala was *all* wolf. June imagined it would be just a matter of time before something triggered her change. "Even with your explanation, I don't understand—how is it possible that I've gone my whole life without knowing this about myself?"

The wolf's eyes dropped. "Everyone is different. Some humans often go their entire lives without discovering their potential or the truth about themselves. Think about that graveyard you were in today. It's full of secrets, most of which were kept from the bearers themselves."

June remembered walking through the barriers in her mind only moments ago. Remembered their parting, like a shroud of clouds. These clouds, while they'd let in plenty of light, had surrounded her thoughts for her entire life. She hadn't even paid much attention to them in the final moments before her change. Now she realized their significance and that they were likely not unique to her.

One of June's long ears rose and twitched, allowing in a symphony of sound, each note with meaning. She recognized it as the clattering of voices that always ran in the background of her mind, white noise she never paid any attention to. The soundtrack of life, crisp and decipherable for the first time. The voices of the wind, murmurings of insects deep in the ground, the breath of small animals dreaming somewhere in the cave's shadows. She heard and recognized each note. This new form came with incredible, expanded sensory perception—beautiful enough to stave off her fears. Strange but amazing. The *how* of it didn't matter. She loved this new reality.

Sorrow chased joy as June lifted a paw and examined it in the starlit darkness of the cave. Even lying here, she could feel the potential. Her body hummed with pure vitality. With each passing second, she could feel her petty human concerns slipping further and further away from a place of importance in her mind.

Spellbound, she had a tremendous urge to spend the remainder of her life exploring this form. At ninety-two, she doubted she had that much more time. A sigh came out that sounded more like a whimper. "My life is almost over. It would have been nice to know this, oh, I don't know, eighty-five years ago."

Jack lay on the ground now in a manner that resembled pictures of the Sphinx. While his gaze intensified, he said nothing.

June let her paw drop to the ground. "Am I already dead?" June asked, suddenly wondering if all of this wasn't some post-death experience.

"Do you *feel* dead?"

June had never felt more alive, disoriented, or frustrated. She was here because of George. But her human life suddenly felt like a dream. Unreal and unimportant. June struggled to make sense of things, which only amplified her frustration. A frustration that was quickly growing from anger into violent rage. A growl erupted from June's chest that surprised even her and made the pups' eyes shoot open. She wanted answers. Now.

Jack backed onto all fours. "Easy there, young one. You're like those pups at your side. Everything is brand new for you. The wolf's rage is animal instinct and you will have to learn to control it. Control is the most important thing for a wolf to master. Remember that your feelings aren't law. You don't have to act on them."

June's canines, which were huge, bared. She stifled a snarl. "I have no patience for riddles."

"I'm sorry. I was trying to give you the information in digestible bits. Too much too soon is never good."

"Stop spoon-feeding and lay it all out there." Ninety-two years as a woman had seen June through more deaths and births than she could count, wars, changes in technology and the earth's surface. Her mind had enough plasticity to handle anything he could throw her way—Yes, and she wanted it all right then. All the sooner to find her husband. "Starting with how this connects to George. Is he like me?"

"Yes and no. No one that we know of is like you. You are Dargin and more than Dargin. Something greater. A blend. What sort? I don't know. None of our pack does. Your parents didn't either."

"My parents? You knew them?" June's head was reeling.

"Yes, your biological parents were part of our pack."

June had long ago made peace with her adoption, although she'd always wondered what circumstances led to her parents giving her up. That was the question that never stopped mattering, even though the weight lessened over the years. But this new information about her parents made her realize that peace had been artificial. "Tell me more!" she demanded.

"Your mother realized right away that you weren't like the rest of us. She wanted to keep you, but your father said your differences made you a target. Any pack who possessed you could enhance the power of their line. He wanted you to choose your mate for yourself. So in the end, they sent you away. But we watched you. We've always been watching you, June. When the enemy pack sniffed you out, we sent George to protect you. You chose him."

June had a million thoughts crashing around in her mind. Her parents had given her up out of love and protection? And sent George to watch over her? She wasn't human and there were others like her? "Are all of George's brothers like him? Like you?"

The wolf nodded. "We are. All twelve of us."

Twelve? "But I thought there were only six?"

"Not everyone agreed with your father's decision to send you off. Some of our brothers and others from the pack shunned us. They've been hunting us—hunting you—ever since."

"Hunting? You mean to say George has been protecting me, protecting this secret for all of these years?"

Jack nodded. June remembered George's vow of protection from all those years ago, the one that preceded his proposal. Boy, she'd had no idea the gravity of those words at the time. "And my parents? You said they were part of your pack. What happened to them?"

Jack's gaze dropped to the floor and a silence fell between them. She sensed any answer he gave would be conjecture. He didn't know. June's heart constricted, and she swallowed down her pain. She knew she would grieve their loss at some point, but first, she had another question. "What makes my blend so unique?"

Jack lifted his gaze. "The best we can make out, somewhere along the centuries, your people mixed with ancient magic. While George and I can change into wolf form only, your mother could take other forms. It was said that far back in her line there'd been women who could speak with the elements, to make them act at their behest."

June thought of her attacker all of those years ago. She'd categorized him as deranged. Afterward, she'd been so sidetracked with her feelings for George that she'd never thought much about the strange words he'd uttered when he reeled from one of her kicks. "When I was young, a man attacked me. He called me wolf-witch. Are you saying that I *am* a witch?"

"It has been said, but I know little about your kind. I believe you have the ability to be even more than that."

"More than that?" Her curiosity was well and truly piqued. "Why?"

"For starters, you're able to communicate with me in both forms. Clearly. Most of us take years to develop cross-species communication, and our abilities are only a fraction of what you've been able to master in minutes."

"I see." June pawed at the ground as her mind returned to thoughts of her attack. The memories invariably turned to the animal who'd rescued her that day. "It was him in the alley all those years ago, wasn't it? George saved my life."

Jack nodded.

And he'd been protecting her ever since. "Where's George?" Her voice trembled with a mix of longing and frustration. "Why isn't he the one here telling me this? Does it have something to do with the Native woman who disappeared?"

Sadness darkened his eyes. "Nobody knows where George is. Sheila Featherstone made the amulets for our pack. When her house burned down, we knew the enemy was close to finding you again after all of these years. George went out to hunt them, but he hadn't changed in decades."

June sighed. So that was why he'd disappeared. "I knew there had to be a good reason."

Jack cocked his head. "You doubted?"

"Never," June said, her voice firm. "What happened after George changed? Did something go wrong?" She dreaded asking the question because she knew the answer was going to hurt.

"The hunt took longer than we planned, years longer, and he hasn't shifted back."

There was more to this story, and June knew it. "What aren't you telling me?"

Jack looked down at the pups, then away.

"Tell me," she insisted. She'd lived all of her life separated from this truth, and she didn't want to waste another second living in ignorance. "Don't spare me any details."

Jack sighed. "He left the pack and went full, lone wolf." The gravity of his tone let her know this was something serious for their kind. "Of all of us, you are the only one who can find him and convince him to remember himself. To come back. And this is why I asked you for his amulet. We need it to help focus him once he's retaken his human form."

She felt another growl rising in her chest. She shifted to quash it. "My entire life has been a lie, and only now that I'm useful to this pack of strangers is the truth being revealed?" Her next question was why in the hell they'd waited so long to find her.

One of the wolf pups nuzzled deeper into June's furry side, releasing a wild, spicy smell of earth and forest. She inhaled. It was a lovely smell. If she left to search for George, who would take care of them? They were so young, and traveling with them would be difficult, especially in the winter weather. How did mother wolves manage?

As if hearing her thoughts, the wolf spoke. "We shouldn't have to travel far. Now that you've taken this form, if we move South, George will feel you and come for you."

"South?"

The wolf nodded, and June didn't bother to ask how he knew. She was suddenly exhausted. Whether from the change or from the information, she couldn't keep her eyes open any longer.

"You are going to be sleepy for a long time. Changing takes massive energy. I'll let you and the cubs rest now. Tomorrow night we'll move toward George."

June didn't want to wait to be reunited with her love, but her body didn't care. Within minutes, she was fast asleep. That night, the whale came to her again in her dreams. This time it was where it belonged, in an ocean.

ELEVEN

June was sitting at the mouth of the cave when the voices came. Her ears pricked, her hackles rose, and her muscles tensed.

Humans.

Jack had just left to go hunting for the night. The plan was to fill their stomachs with something small before they went to look for George. The pups, noting her change in demeanor, stopped playing behind her and stilled.

"It looks like she came through here," a man said.

Damn, it was Hank. Of course he and Aza would be looking for her. And she hadn't been at all careful when she'd been following Jack the night before. Hank wasn't a bad tracker but even if he were, she'd left enough of a trail to lead him right to her.

Scenting the air and rotating her ears, June calculated that they were at least a mile out. She could run away with the cubs and pray Jack would be able to follow their trail, or she could hunker down deeper into the cave and wait for Hank and Aza to arrive. She didn't imagine Hank would keep Aza out much after dark. The sun was nearly down, making it hard for him to follow any trail.

June thought about transforming into human form. If she could speak to her daughter maybe that would be enough to stop their search. She closed her eyes. She grit her teeth. She curled her toes, squeezing each and every muscle until it cramped. But no matter how hard she tried, she couldn't make the shift.

Nature exhaled, the breeze lifting her whiskers, and June realized that panic had stilted her breath. Would she be trapped in this form forever? She couldn't do anything about it at the moment. Time was moving quickly, and catching the occasional word let June know Hank was moving quickly, too—in her direction.

June scanned the cave. On the back wall, a crawl space led deeper into the hill. There was little likelihood Hank or Aza would go scouring the dark cave, even if they did find it. June grabbed the first pup by the scruff of his neck and securely tucked it away, then came back for the second, making sure they were both perfectly concealed. Neither of them wriggled out or tried to follow. Further proof in June's mind that the cubs were smart and attuned to her emotionally.

"Don't move," she growled quietly, just in case. Then she scooped up her robe—the only evidence of her presence that was left—and ran out of the cave.

The power in her legs felt amazing. Even in her youth, she'd never experienced anything comparable. Such speed. Such strength. It was exhilarating beyond comprehension. Never had she known such freedom. Like the scent of the pups, she was all wild, all forest.

Her paws were like springboards. She leapt over boulders and across the creek, and still felt like she was holding back. She could do this forever, to the end of the continent. Last night Jack had told her that she could take any shape she wanted. Did that mean she could fly? At the water's edge, she would grow wings and keep going. Motion was life and June Chambray wanted to live in the euphoria that was her animal self until she drew her last breath. Suddenly, she understood why George hadn't shifted back.

George.

The thought of him was a siren's call, crystallizing her thoughts and purpose. *George.* He was the reason she was running. To get away from Hank and Aza and get to him. That was her focus right now. Later, she could chase the wind or fly high on its currents. But first, she had to take care of Hank and Aza. If she moved quickly enough, she might be able to get them to veer away from the trail she'd left last night by circling back and creating a new one that led in a different direction.

June retraced her footsteps from the night before, coming perilously close to the humans. At Dargin Lake, instead of going left, as she had before, she went right, but not too far. There, she left her robe, in the tall cattails on the edge of the water. She slipped into the lake quietly. The icy water didn't penetrate until she'd nearly reached the bank on the other side, where she crouched in a thicket of shrubs listening as the humans drew nearer.

Twenty minutes later, a flashlight split the dark. "Look!" It was Aza. "She was here. This is her robe."

In the faint light, June could see Hank bend down and pick the robe up. He examined it under the ray of his flashlight. "I don't see any blood on it, or any tears. You think she just came out here and took it off?"

Aza stepped to the water's edge. "I do. Just before she jumped in." She brought the robe to her heart and cried, "Oh, Hank! Did we push her to this?"

Stark pain in her daughter's voice made June want to reveal herself. The fresh anguish of recently discovering she'd been living a lie amplified June's pain at seeing her daughter blaming herself for her mother's supposed death. But June didn't know how to return to her human form yet, and even if she did, she wouldn't until she'd found George. Once she did, he was going to be the one to explain all of this to their daughter and granddaughter. There was no way June would let her progeny go through their entire lifetimes without knowing of their true identities. No, her girls would know their power and as much of their history as they could, as soon as she could get back to them.

Hank put his arm around Aza, practically pulling her off her feet. "No, she wouldn't have done anything that drastic. Come on Babe, there's got to be another explanation. We should call the police. I don't know if they'll search tonight or what. But we need to get help."

TWELVE

"We'll rest at dawn," June said, turning her back on Jack and walking to the edge of a mountainside cliff. Still in her wolf form, the moon, tucked high in the night sky, called to her. It also indicated at least two more hours until sunrise. Moving at a steady trot, Jack, June, and the cubs had made it to the Kentucky border. Jack had suggested they stop twice already, but June refused.

It wasn't just her wolf form that propelled her. Now that she'd confirmed George was alive, she could feel him pulling her like a magnet. If it hadn't been for the cubs' need to feed, June wouldn't have stopped until they were reunited. At one point, she'd contemplated leaving them with Jack. He could find a way to care for them. Almost as soon as she'd had the thought, one pup looked up from licking his paw with pleading golden eyes, and she knew there was no way she could leave them.

As they continued on, foggy mists started to roll through the dense forest, shrouding the land with an eerie quiet. Finally, they came to a mountain pass where the Kentucky hills rippled into the Tennessee border. The pup in June's mouth grew restless, whining. She opened her jaws and Luna, she'd named the girl, toppled out, landing on her feet. June lay down and rolled onto her side. Both pups latched onto her teats in seconds.

"They need to rest. They can't rest properly when we carry them," Jack said.

He was right. She was just about to tell him so when the sound of a twig snapping had Jack at attention, scenting the air. He looked at her and shook his head. She knew at once that he couldn't make out the scent. Neither could she.

A chill ran down June's spine. Though a wolf for not even two days, she'd already become so attuned to the sounds and scents of the wild, she knew anything that got close without alerting their olfactory senses was powerfully dangerous. Some latent animal understanding, she supposed.

Luna had unlatched from June's teat to stand statue still, growling at something unseen in a nearby grove of aspens. Clouds broke, and the moon crept through, illuminating the aspens' white tops like bones in a graveyard. June knew that whatever crouched in the dark shrubs at their base was a threat.

"Stay here. I'll go see what it is," Jack said.

There was no way June would let Jack go by himself. She nosed the reluctant cubs away from her chest and lifted them into the crevice of a tree, high enough to hopefully keep them from harm's way. Then she crept closer to Jack, her back to his, her golden eyes scanning the dark forest.

"I told you to stay," Jack snarled. "This isn't a game, and you aren't ready."

He may have been right, but something inside her wouldn't, couldn't back down. "You said yourself, I have strong animal impulses."

A low growl cut their sniping short. Exhilaration coursed through June's veins, hot and battle-ready. It'd been ages since she'd fought and never with the power of a wolf. The idea of combat in this form excited her.

In addition to whipping up her adrenaline, the sound of the growl narrowed down the location of their mystery opponent. He was behind the shrubs to June's right. Detecting this, Jack placed himself between her and the other animal, growling back.

June knew she should let Jack keep the lead, but her senses were going wild and, with each passing second, she was getting a stronger impression of what the animal lurking in the shadows was thinking. It was a male. An *angry* male. Though she couldn't see him with her eyes, she could see him in her mind, venomous drool dripping from canines he planned to sink deep into Jack's neck.

Without thinking, June leapt through the dark night and over Jack. Surrendering to her instincts, she let out a vicious growl when she landed on the back of the other wolf, claws first. Twice as large as Jack, three times as large as her, he tried to buck her off, but size didn't matter. June had something that was stronger than muscle or years of battle training—love, and she held fast, sinking her jaws deep into the wolf's shoulder blade. The animal howled. It was a blood-curdling sound of pain, far deeper than physical, so wrought with anguish that her own heart constricted.

Whirling fast and then stopping faster, he threw her from his back. She landed with a thud on the ground, the air knocked from her lungs. In an instant, the massive wolf was on top of her, fangs bared. One blue eye and one green eye blazing with bloodthirsty anger. One blue eye and one green eye...so familiar and yet so strange all at once. In an instant, memories of waking up to those smiling eyes flooded her with a love so thick she could scarcely breathe. She would know those eyes anywhere.

He hovered over her. June was sure he recognized her, too, even though he'd never seen her in this form before. The air pulsed between them with that radiant electricity that always marked their connection. It made her chest stiffen with hope and desire. *He must feel it too!*

He sniffed, his wet nose grazing her neck. Then he pulled back again, a question in his eyes. A yearning too.

"George?" June sat up on her elbows, suddenly transformed into human form. Naked in the grass, she reached for him. "George!" she exclaimed.

Jack leapt to her side, swiping George's head in the process, leaving a thick gash from his ear to his chin. Suddenly, George's eyes turned into murderous daggers, showing no sign of recognition—only rage. He growled with nearly enough force to rip bark from the surrounding trees.

Jack, close enough that she could feel the heat of his body as well as a whisper of fear, had wedged himself between her and

George. Jack was so much smaller than George. Her George, any glimmer of recognition now extinguished, blinded as he was by some all-consuming rage and animalistic kill instinct.

George sprang from his crouching position high into the air where he met Jack head on. Both crashed to the earth. George slashed at Jack's throat with claws and monstrous fangs.

Naked and suddenly feeling like a stranger in her own body, June struggled to stand, desperate to intervene. Even in the dark night, she could see Jack's crimson blood everywhere. Panicked, June screamed. The sound brought the sleeping canopy of leaves overhead to life. Hundreds of grackles swooped down from the branches, diving one after another toward George's head. Their claws swiped at him, coming dreadfully close to his eyes. Those blasted eyes—sensitive but unseeing in the way that mattered most to June.

Initially, George fought on without pausing to confront the birds. But when batch after batch discharged like cannon fodder against his head, back and arms, he had no choice but to take them on too. Obviously distracted, his energy and focus divided between the birds covering him now like a writhing blanket and Jack, George lost the advantage of his strength.

Swiping at a pillow of birds surrounding his head, George was caught unawares by Jack. He grabbed George's neck and slammed him against the ground in a perfectly orchestrated move that left George unconscious, his head and neck at an odd angle. Panting, Jack collapsed into a heap of exhaustion at George's feet.

"What have you done?" she cried.

George stiffened and glanced at the birds as though afraid they might attack him. "Don't worry, it looks worse than it is."

But June *was* worried. Her stomach in knots, she crept to George's side, hesitating before bringing her fingers to his head and rubbing the coarse, thick fur. In four years she'd imagined their reunion, dreamed up all kinds of scenarios, but never this.

"Why did you attack him?" She could scarcely control her rage.

Jack shifted into his human form. "He didn't recognize either one of us."

"He did. I saw it."

"Not really. I know he paused, but his tail told me he was going to attack." Jack lifted his hands, calling for calm. "He's been in his wolf form for too long. His human memories are repressed. But they still came through."

Her brow furrowed. She didn't understand.

"The longer a wolf spends in this form, the stronger he becomes. And George is an Alpha. He could have killed us both. Believe it or not, he was holding himself back. Part of his rage came from seeing me with you, but not even he understood that."

June let her fingers trail from the edge of his ear to his massive jaw. The explanation made sense. "Thank God for the birds."

"I think we have you to thank for that. You notice how they only came down around George? They were protecting you." Jack reached around the back of his neck and snapped off the amulet he wore on a chain around it. Then wound it around George's front legs.

Watching him, a memory came to June of that day, so many years ago, when she'd been attacked. George grimaced, and she remembered how the cuffs her attacker had thrown on her had nearly immobilized her with her own feelings of anger. Her heart constricted. "What did you just do to him?"

"I put my collar on him. It's a wolf's equivalent to a wand. It lets us harness our power. Manage our own shifts. If you place your collar on another wolf, you can contain their power by bending it back toward them. I can also force his shift."

"But won't he just break it when he comes to?" That's what she'd done those years ago.

"It's not possible for one wolf to break another's collar. It's the ultimate domination, usually the prelude to death. That's why using your own collar on another is rarely done."

"Not possible to break? But I broke one when I was just a girl."

Jack nodded his head slowly as he eyed her from head to toe. "As I said before, you are different. This is why the pack wanted you to begin with. You and your line cannot be contained."

"I see." Suddenly June had an image of herself being passed around like breeding livestock. Revulsion then fear shook her. "Thank God that's no longer a threat."

Jack hung his head low.

"You did eliminate the threat, didn't you?"

"We weren't able to overpower them all."

"You weren't able to overpower them all? That means my daughter and granddaughter are still at risk. Do any of you ever tell the full truth?" June made to leave. There was no way she could let her girls fall into the hands of whoever was left of this enemy pack.

"Where is the enemy?"

"I don't know, but he might. What we need to do now is get him back to his own amulet. It will help to restore his memories." Jack was crouching over George, now in his human form, too, but looking years younger than he had the last time she'd seen him.

She wanted to ask about this but didn't have time. Concern for her girls nearly crippled her. "Yes, we do, and fast."

Instead of doing what June always did, taking out her metal bit and drilling a deep hole into which she'd pitch her feelings, June channeled them. She wanted to get George and the cubs home fast. But she needed to get back to her daughter and granddaughter.

June imagined a peregrine falcon. Seconds later, she flapped her wings.

Jack looked at her, his eyes round. "What have you done? How is that..." June gathered from his inability to speak that though he knew it was possible, seeing it done jarred him.

She lifted a wing. "I'm beginning to understand why I was able to call them," she mused.

He shook his head slowly, clearly still thrown by her transformation. It seemed to unnerve him, too. Perhaps it had to do with having just seen the birds' power unleashed. She studied him. It was more than that. People were often uncomfortable with another's rapid ascent. Could that be it?

"Well, you don't have to stay like that," he finally said. "Now that we have him, we can travel in human form. I'll call the pack. Let them know where we are. They'll take us back."

"I don't have that long. I need to get back to my girls. To protect them."

Jack shook his head. "I don't think it's a good idea for you to shift alone, June. Shifting isn't easy. You saw what happened to George, and he's been doing this for hundreds of years."

She wanted to know more about that, but now wasn't the time. She simply looked away, and said, "Yeah, well I'm not George."

THIRTEEN

The sound of his own teeth chattering brought George into consciousness. Icy wind bore down on his bare cheeks, nearly numb from the cold. Exposed and pissed about it, he jerked upright, but not nearly as quickly as he'd planned. His movements were slow and heavy, gravity acting on him like an alien force, pressing him flat against a cushioned back seat of what he gradually realized was a moving vehicle. He didn't need to look down to know he was back in his human form. This level of cold shooting in from the open window never would have bothered his wolf, or even the man he was fifty years ago, when he changed regularly.

Domestication had weakened him. George snorted in disgust.

Images of last night's defeat came back to him in slow motion. Each frame gave rise to more anger. In a fair fight, he wouldn't be sitting here. Wrists collar-bound, fire-hot flames of pain shot up his forearms, into his chest and shoulders. His head felt like a butcher's mallet had cleaved it. The more pissed he got, the heavier the weight that oppressed him.

Still, even in human form, his wolf was too strong not to fight, so he did, tugging against the restraints until his wrists bled. He would have sliced his own hands off if the restraints would have allowed it.

A large man wearing a thick scarf wound around his neck and a shiny black blazer drove the speeding car. He reeked of new money and self-importance. Next to him, a muscular man in a blue fleece and skullcap dozed with his head on the tinted window. George made to slip his tethered wrists around the driver's neck, but the cuffs stopped him before he raised his arms midway, sending a searing pain through his body.

George moaned.

The driver looked at the passenger, who'd opened his eyes. "Sleeping Beauty's up. Keep an eye on him. If that wretched stink's any indication, he's been wild so long he probably doesn't even know his own name, let alone recognize us."

Smug suit guy was partially right. George remembered his own name, but the guys up front were a mystery. And he definitely stank. Good, he hoped it made them both sick.

The passenger turned around in his seat to look at George. "You don't recognize us, do you?" George recognized his emotions. The guy's grey eyes looked stunned and hurt. Whoever he was, they had meant something to each other once.

George looked away and tried to keep his teeth from chattering. He was wearing a silky button-down and slacks. He didn't remember much about himself, but he knew for sure these fancy clothes weren't his, and they definitely weren't heavy enough for this weather. Damn, he missed his wolf. He'd be back in his form soon enough, once he figured out how to ditch these bastards.

"We're your brothers," the hurt-looking guy said. "Two of them, at least. The others are going to meet us. I'm Jack, and this is Keith." Jack jabbed his thumb in Keith's direction. Keith continued to stare out of the windshield at the empty road ahead. "I know I'm wasting my breath, but it's no use struggling," Jack said, watching him closely.

"Definitely wasting your breath," Keith said, scowling.

"Fuck you," George growled, realizing the collar around his wrists smelled like Jack.

He'd done this. So much for that whole 'the eyes are the windows to the soul' garbage. As soon as George was loose, he'd make Jack pay. Keith too, just for being there. The sun was coming up on the right side of the car. They were headed north. He'd figure out what to do next when they stopped, or maybe sooner, if only his teeth would stop chattering long enough for him to hear himself think. God, he felt so vulnerable in this human form.

"He's freezing. Roll up the windows and turn up the heat," Jack said.

"No way. Bad enough I had to give him my clothes. I'll never get the stink out of them now." Keith smoothed the breast of his suit, then gripped the wheel with black leather gloves. "I'm not ruining my Armani, too, brother or not."

"No brother of mine would ever have done this," George shot a murderous glance up front, wincing when the rage reverse-flowed into him.

"Ingrate!" Keith spat out. He still hadn't met his gaze in the rearview mirror, and George knew it was out of pure self-preservation. If they made eye contact, Keith would probably be moved to act violently. And though George's memories were foggy, somehow he knew some code prohibited striking another while restrained. "You betrayed the pack."

Yes. Pack code. That was why his so-called brother wasn't pummeling him.

"And do you have any idea the pain you've caused June and the girls?" Keith demanded.

June.... Suddenly, George's mind flooded with images of the wolf from last night and the beautiful woman she'd changed into.

"Easy, Keith. It's not like he did it on purpose. His collar was torn during battle."

Keith fixed his eyes on Jack. "How many times have you 'lost' your collar during battle?"

"So that's the standard? Since it hasn't happened to either of us it's impossible? You sound like a human. Now roll up your window before I make you do it." Jack's voice was strong and it was clear that in the pack order, Jack's rank was higher because Keith didn't look like the type to back down to anyone under ordinary circumstances.

George liked the way Jack thought, even though he didn't need anyone defending him. And he was grateful when the window went up, and the cold air stopped blasting his face.

His brothers lapsed into a stony silence, another blessing as he tried to order his thoughts. Why did the name *June* have such an impact on him, and what had happened to his own collar? Until now, both had been lost to the passions of his animal mind. But now that he was back in human form, his heart ached at the mere mention of this woman. He also knew that only the collar would help him to fill in blanks eating at his mind.

FOURTEEN

"Where have you been? I thought you were dead!" Aza practically shouted, causing both Luna and Luke—she'd decided on the boy cub's name at last—to growl, protectively.

"Shh, it's okay," June said to the cubs at her ankles before meeting Aza's astonished gaze. Relief swelled June's heart as she took in the sight of her daughter, red-faced and angry, and her granddaughter standing at her side, wearing a bemused expression. Aza could rant and rave all she wanted. They were safe, and that was all June cared about.

"Kentucky," June said simply, stepping back from the door and waving her girls inside. Luna and Luke followed, their ears twitching with curiosity.

Zala stepped forward, her dark brown eyes sparkling conspiratorially as she wrapped her grandmother into a big hug, pulling her close to whisper in her ear, "Good for you, Grans." June rubbed her hand through the girl's thick black hair. It'd grown longer and she even more beautiful in her months abroad. Travel had been good for her.

"Is that where these two cuties came from? They're adorable," Zala said, bending down to greet the pups.

"Kentucky? Kentucky! What on earth possessed you to go there?" Aza's high-pitched scream interrupted Zala's introduction to the wolf cubs. "I thought we had an agreement. I came back and you'd just disappeared. You didn't even have the courtesy to leave a note. You left the door wide open. I found your robe at the edge of the lake!" Aza threw her hands up in the air and let out a shrill, exasperated cry, leaving June even more grateful for Zala's initial words of comfort.

"I'm sorry you worried," June said, remembering her anguish at seeing her daughter blaming herself when she thought June used the pond as a watery grave.

"Sorry? No. I don't accept that! You don't get to make me think you're dead and then just shrug it off with an apology. Wandering away without telling anyone is a serious problem and the police think so too. And this!" Aza gestured toward the pups. "Don't even get me started on you bringing two puppies into the house. Do you honestly think I'd let you bring them to live in my house?"

As though sensing it'd be better to let the humans talk alone, Luna and Luke scurried upstairs.

Eyebrows arched, June walked to the kitchen and grabbed her teapot from the stove. If it was going to be one of those visits, which it clearly was, she needed some lavender chamomile to sustain her. She turned on the water. The glass she'd broken the night she left was no longer in the sink. Aza must have cleaned it. The woman never met a mess she couldn't sanitize. Too bad she took the same approach to her life.

Though June understood Aza's reaction today, she couldn't help but think her daughter would have a lot more fun in life if she'd just embrace the messy every now and then. It was as if Aza had somehow inherited a bundle of fears June didn't even realize she had. June thought about the man who'd attacked her all those years ago, a man from what she now knew was an enemy pack. Had her daughter somehow picked up on George's subconscious fear that the pack would one day find their family? Or the fear June had about the first battle not being her last?

June sighed and put the full teapot back onto the stove, a small hiss releasing as the gas fired.

"I don't want any tea, Mom. I'm ready to go. Please, just fill some bags and let's go back to my house. Your new room is all ready."

Without even waiting, Aza went upstairs and came back down a few minutes later carrying a duffle bag. She let it fall at her mother's feet. "Here. This should be everything you need. We can come back later for the rest. But those dogs are going to have to go to the pound."

June turned to face her daughter and folded her arms over her chest, her long gray braid falling straight down her back. "I'm not going anywhere. Neither are Luna and Luke. Your father will be home shortly, and he will explain things."

Aza gasped. "My *father*? Mom, I thought we discussed this already. You just said—"

"I just said that your father can explain things." Like a proxy for June's rising frustration, the tea kettle steamed and whistled. June turned off the stove and set about pouring three cups.

Zala, who'd been watching from the kitchen table without saying anything, finally spoke, "Mom, the puppies can stay with me. And I don't know why you're so set on bringing Grans to your house this instant. If she wants us to stay here, let's just stay here for a little while longer."

Aza whipped around to face her daughter. "Waiting for *Dad* to materialize out of thin air? We've indulged in this lunacy long enough. Besides, young lady, this is an adults-only conversation. You don't have a seat at this table."

Zala stood. "First of all, I'm thirty-two. Second of all, it's not a table if there's only one leg. That's called a pedestal." Aza gasped, but Zala was clearly just getting started. She came to stand next to June. "Don't you even see the hypocrisy here? Child must obey the parent?" Zala moved her index finger from her to her mother and then landed on June.

It took a beat for Aza to find her voice as she stared at her daughter incredulously. June had to say, she was a bit surprised that someone finally stood up to Aza. "I can't believe..." Aza's voice trailed.

"What?" Zala lifted her hands palm up. "Good friends and family should be each other's mirrors. Show you who you are before you go out into the world with your ugly face on. And I love you, Mom, but you're being really ugly right now." Zala's tone was tender but her words were firm.

June was incredibly proud of the combination.

But Aza wasn't. June could see the defensive walls rise immediately. Aza thrust her hands on her hips. "I should have called the police the second I got here." Aza started for the phone on the kitchen wall. "They've been searching for you for two days. When they see how irresponsible you've been, they'll understand why you have to come live with me."

"The police? Are you seriously trying to pull that card right now? Why? You're only going to make things worse if you do that," Zala said, stepping in front of her mother.

"Out of my way, young lady. I am the mother here."

"Actually, *I* am the mother." June sprang across the kitchen, and when she landed, it was on all fours in wolf form.

"Holy shit!" Zala's hands flew to her mouth.

Aza froze, her mouth agape, the scent of her fear drenching the room.

"If I'd known that was all it took, I would have done that forty minutes ago," June said, looking from her daughter to granddaughter.

Zala, always open-minded, recovered first. "Wow, Grandma. I always knew you were a powerful woman, but this is next level!" Her eyes grew to the size of twin eagle eggs. "Wait, I understand you?"

A line of wonder etched between June's whiskered brows. Was Zala's ability to communicate without even shifting an indication of the power she would display once she did? "You're my granddaughter. There's probably not anything I can do that you can't and better, and that includes using your wolf to speak with mine."

Zala smiled. "I have a wolf?

June shifted back into human form, throwing a blanket over her shoulders before gently nudging her shocked daughter into an armchair in the living room. "Probably, my dear. Probably. And we'll talk about that later. Right now, I need you to help me with your mother. Go get a washcloth from the bathroom. Run it under some cold water first," June said as she knelt beside her daughter.

Zala hesitated before running into the back of the house.

"How did you do that? And how long have you known that you could?" a blanched Aza finally stuttered.

"My poor baby girl. What did I do to make you cling so tightly to these conventions of yours?" June whispered as she pushed Aza's long black hair away from her face.

"Conventions? I just watched my mother turn into a wolf and back, and you're condemning my shock as conventional? Where'd you get your motherly instincts? A clearance sale?"

June laughed and, this time, so did Aza. "Now will you believe me when I say your father will be here soon to explain everything?"

Aza nodded. "My head is hard but not impenetrable."

June kissed Aza's forehead. "That's okay, sweetie. I love your hard side and soft side."

Zala came back with a cold washcloth. "So you finally made up?" Zala smiled as June took the cloth and folded it in three, laying it flat on her daughter's forehead.

"Possibly," June said, quirking her head mischievously.

Zala nodded. "Those aren't just regular puppies upstairs, are they Grans?"

June smiled. They most definitely weren't. Somehow, the wolves had managed to make it to her home before Jack and George. Upset, he'd called to let her know that George tried to escape when they stopped, freeing the pups. She'd been worried about them in the wild until they appeared on her porch earlier. "No more regular than you and I."

"Wow. I thought I came back from my trip with some adventure tales." Zala sat on the couch. "You've got to explain."

"Yeah, what she said." Aza indicated her chin toward Zala as she pressed the damp cloth to her forehead.

"I want to. But it's a long story, and unfortunately, I don't have all the answers. I promise, we'll all have them shortly. For now, I need you to sit tight a little bit longer. Trust me," June said, smiling as she left her girls in stunned silence while she went outside to the front porch.

George would be there soon. She could feel him coming close. He would be able to explain things better—to all of them.

***

Twenty minutes later, June was sitting in her rocker when a black Range Rover came tearing up the road in front of her farmhouse. Though June was expecting trouble, she knew this wasn't it.

The truck turned into her driveway and stopped close to the house. The driver's side and passenger's side doors sprung open, and two huge men lumbered out of the front seats. June recognized Jack and Keith immediately. Jack went round to the back of the car and opened the door. June could hear angry muttering from inside as he dragged George out and to his feet.

Once outside of the truck, June drank in the sight of him. The first thing she noticed, other than the fact that George dwarfed both of his tall brothers, were his bound hands. June remembered her own binding and winced for George. At the very least, he was uncomfortable. If the scowl on his face was any indication, his anger was eating him up from the inside.

The long time spent in his wolf form had changed him. Muscular and bulky before, his body was sinewy now. And while he'd left her grey, his face beginning to show the marks of age, he'd returned to her a man who looked no older than thirty-five. Whether from the time roaming free or the collar-forced shift, she didn't know. His hair was once again the blue-black it'd been when they first met. There was a wildness in his eyes, but instead of detracting from his looks, it added to them, giving him a more rugged air. Even though the tingling nerves of self-consciousness about their apparent age difference heated her cheeks, everything else inside of June wanted to run to him, flung herself into his arms, and taste his lips.

But George would barely make eye contact. Was her older appearance off-putting to him? She suspected she could have shifted into a younger version of herself but, until this moment, she'd seen no need.

A tug from Jack sent George stepping forward. June's heart constricted as she watched his slow, suspicious movements. Again, maybe it was discomfort from the bindings, but he seemed to be preoccupied with his wingtips. Well, the wingtips on his feet. Keith, the dandy of the group, no doubt selected the change of clothing from his own closet for George to wear. George had always been a simple man, partial to T-shirts, flannels, and Timberlands. The person standing before her was only a shell of her George, who normally would have taken her in his arms and given her a kiss that left her toes curling after such a long separation. June wondered if he remembered her at all.

"Come on, let's go inside and give them a little privacy," Jack motioned to Keith to follow. Jack was always the more sensitive of the six brothers.

Keith spun to face Jack. "That's putting a lot of faith in that collar. Don't ya think?"

"Naw, my faith is in her," Jack responded, his admiring gaze landing on June.

"If you say so," Keith grumbled and turned to June. "Don't do anything stupid. He's still a lot more animal than man."

Ignoring Keith's sharp tone, June nodded and gave both of the men a little smile of gratitude as they walked past her into the house.

A beat passed before either of them spoke. June swallowed.

"I saved your seat," she finally called down to George, motioning to the chair beside her. How long had she prayed for this moment? Envisioned them sitting side by side in these chairs once again. In each daydream and fantasy they'd always picked up just where they'd left off. She'd never thought about the accounting they'd have to do. And never in her wildest author imaginings had she contemplated accounting for a magical lineage and rabid enemies who wanted to breed her and the girls like they were plantation stock in the 1800s.

George looked up and held her gaze. June held her breath, worried that he might not come to her. For the first time in all of their years together, she had no clue what he was thinking or feeling. It scared her.

Only when he finally took the first step toward her, did June realize how long of a road they actually had to go. It would take time for them to get back to where they used to be and maybe they would never get exactly back to where they once were—but it didn't matter to her as long as they were together.

In the time it took for George to get from the side of the car to the seat on the porch, June transformed into a younger version of herself. She felt uncomfortable greeting this man who appeared so many decades younger than her with an older woman's face. Catching a glimpse of her black hair and smooth skin in the window, she decided she now looked no more than a shapely woman of forty.

His lips curled into a faint smile as he took the seat beside her, and she gathered that he liked what he saw. June's heart fluttered in her chest—but there was a weight to it. She wondered if he'd smile at her in her natural state. Not wanting to ruin the moment, she pushed that doubt aside.

"I have something that belongs to you." She reached into her coat pocket and pulled out George's amulet. His eyes glittered as they fell to it.

June rose and stood in front of George. He leaned his head toward her, his soft black hair brushing against her hand as she reached around his neck, clasping the chain.

Almost at once, his shoulders expanded. "Ahhh," he sighed and rolled his head.

"Feels better?" June asked.

"Like that first sip of water after wandering dry earth for, oh, I don't know... eternity?"

"I wanted to be that for you."

"You're the hope that kept this lost wanderer going. And even though I'd forgotten, here." He pointed to his head. "I knew it *here*." He pointed to his heart.

Still, his hands remained bound. June remembered what Jack had told her about wolves not being able to break another wolf's collar. He'd told her they needed to keep George restrained until his memories came back, and they could be sure he was no longer a danger. Surely, he was safe.

She looked into his eyes now. They were calmer than they had been when he'd first stepped onto the porch.

"Thank you. You've been holding this seat for a long time," he said.

"That I have. That I have." And because it had been too long, June did the one thing Jack had told her not to do. She'd never been very good at following orders.

She broke George's bindings.

Watching his reaction was like seeing someone glimpse the sun for the first time. A brightness came over him that almost made her squint. It was dazzling and beautiful—and suddenly, she understood why Jack had told her George needed time to be tamed. Otherwise, like any wild, beautiful thing, he would run again.

FIFTEEN

It had been two days since George had come home. June spent much of that time sprucing up the house and trying to get to know her husband again. She'd gone to the market and picked up a bouquet of fall flowers along with several bags of groceries. In a classic "fake it till you make it" move, she'd even pulled out some holiday decorations in her efforts to restore the coziness they'd enjoyed in their home and their lives before his disappearance. A topic about which they'd yet to speak, though not for her lack of trying. What little he did seem to remember, George refused to discuss.

She cooked elaborate meals of lamb, steak, and chicken, hoping to keep the hunger she saw in his dark eyes at bay. There was a restlessness in him that hadn't been there before. She was now glad the papers had been cleared—they might have triggered him. He'd take long walks in the woods, and each time the door closed behind him, June felt her blood run cold. Worry was a constant companion.

Maybe I should have listened to Jack and kept the collar in place longer...

Whereas before, things between them had been sure, now they felt fraught with uncertainty. June grabbed mitts from the hook near the oven and slipped them over her hands. She bent over and pulled open the door. The fragrant aroma of BBQ ribs floated out on a cloud of steam.

"Smells delicious. How much longer?" George asked.

June smiled. At least that hadn't changed. The man still loved her cooking.

She closed the door, stood, and re-homed her oven mitts on a hook above the counter. As she did, large hands wrapped around her waist from behind. Her body thrummed instantly. George ran his fingers along the tips of her suddenly hard nipples and squeezed, lightly.

"*Ah*," she said, relaxing into his touch, her head leaning back onto his chest. His hands slid down her sides.

The desire in his touch warmed every inch of her skin. He gripped her hips and pulled them to his, holding her backside against his groin, grinding as he let out a throaty groan. He steered her to the kitchen table. In seconds, he'd hiked her dress around her hips and had her panties on the floor.

His breath was hot against her neck, sending flames shooting down her breasts and scorching her core. When George was in this mood, one look had her wet. Moves like this left her in a puddle.

George got down on his knees, twisting her to face him, and put his head between her legs, keeping it there until June sang out with pleasure. If they'd had neighbors close by, the wives surely would have looked at their own husbands as though they didn't measure up.

The next several times they had sex were like this: George mounting her from behind, full of hunger and need. June enjoyed herself, but missed the days of tender lovemaking.

Since his return, George had stayed in a younger form. She assumed it was because the youthful vitality made him feel closer to his wolf, happier, so June had remained young as well. Sex with their young bodies was satisfying and fun, but it felt as though their avatars were consorting—not them. The concern that he wouldn't be as attracted to her in her real form nagged her.

In the second week home, June awoke in the middle of the night. She rolled over and reached her hand out— the other side of the bed was empty. Her chest constricted. June sat up. The room was empty. Listening for the sound of water running in the bathroom and hearing nothing, she scanned the hallway for a glimmer of light leaking out from under the bathroom door. Empty as well.

Fearing George had pulled another vanishing act, she slipped on a robe and headed downstairs. As her slippered foot left the bottom stair, an odd tranquility descended. She'd weathered his first disappearance and in that time she'd discovered a side of herself that now left her certain she could go on without him if she had to. Though, of course, that wasn't her preference.

A bitter breeze swirled in the foyer, gliding across her cheek. The front door was ajar. June pulled her robe tighter and stepped onto the porch. There, she found George in his chair, staring out at the cornfields thinking,. It had snowed the night before and a few inches dusted the ground like powdered sugar.

"It's cold out here," she said, shivering and closing the door behind her. If she'd been thinking she would have put on the kettle, or grabbed a coat.

He looked up slowly. "We can control that, to a certain extent, slow down our metabolism so the cold doesn't affect us. You can probably do it better than me since you can manage your shifts without a collar."

"Yeah, Jack told me it was because of my Dargin blood." The look on George's face made her regret mentioning his brother, and she quickly redirected the conversation. "It would be nice to be able to endure the cold without discomfort. Please show me," she said, sitting down in the chair beside him.

George hesitated. June wanted to kick herself for bringing up Jack. She opened her mouth again, part teeth chattering, and part prelude to a new question, but George cut her off before she spoke. He pointed to his head. "Remember when I told you this was your toolbox and you could put anything in it that you wanted?"

June nodded, relieved to see he was moving on.

"See it as a coal, red hot. Let it roll down your back, your arms, let it shatter in your navel and shower blazing cinders down your thighs, coming to rest at your toes."

She saw it all happening as George spoke. Her skin heated, then warmed. "It worked," she said, unwrapping her arms from her body and smiling over at him. "Guess I have a lot to learn. What more can you teach me, sensei?"

Guarded hope glimmered in George's eyes. "You wanna learn, huh?"

"Of course I want to learn. What would make you think otherwise?"

George nodded toward the house. "Ever since I came back, you've been obsessed with cooking and living that damn cookie-cutter life. You haven't uttered a word about your time as a wolf. I figured you were just trying to bury that savage part of you."

June looked down at her feet. So that's what was going on. He was making assumptions about her thoughts, and she was making assumptions about his. "I don't understand. Why didn't you just ask me?"

George's eyes turned stony, and a tinge of melancholy colored his gruff voice. "I don't know. Maybe I've forgotten how to have conversations like that, assuming I ever knew how."

A wistful smile touched her lips as she recalled the past. "Oh, you definitely knew how. You were never one to hold back your opinion or emotions. They flowed out of you honest and unfiltered, without any pretense, unlike anyone I'd ever met before. Looking back, I should have known you couldn't be completely human." She laughed. "Anyway, I was just trying to give you space and time."

George's eyes gleamed with a feral yearning. "Space. I miss space. But not the kind you're thinking of. I miss space as a wolf.

I miss running through the untamed wilderness. I miss being *free*."

June understood. She'd watched the birds soar with a jealous heart. There were times when her skin seemed to itch, a relentless itch that made her want to tear it all off, and she knew it was her falcon crying for a shift. She hadn't because she was afraid that if she flew, she'd come back to an empty nest.

"Why don't you take your wolf form?" she asked, her tone no doubt reflecting the longing she, too, held.

George shook his head. "It's not a good idea. Much as he pissed me off, I probably never would have come back if Jack hadn't collared me. But I'm glad I did," he said, taking her hand.

His touch felt heavy, but not in a good way. The words cut, deep into her soul. He remembered more than he'd let on. He'd been forced to come back in more ways than one. Even though she'd known this on some level, hearing the words aloud made them more real. She hadn't been enough to make George come back. There was something stronger in his life than her. Something that could bring him happiness in ways she would never be able to. The wolf held his devotion like a wife, making June no more than a mistress.

But that was too simplistic, wasn't it? Guilt, resentment, and love blended into a sharp knife that twisted in June's gut. She was no mistress. She was simply a woman making him choose between life and death; their domestic life at the expense of his wolf.

A shudder wracked her shoulders, and George must have seen out of the corner of his eye. "Come, there's another way to protect you from the cold." He pulled her onto his lap, his heat radiating through his flannel pajamas. His warmth enveloped her, growing more intense by the second. She leaned down and brushed her lips against his. All at once, his arousal pressed against her hip and his grip tightened. "Let's take this inside."

June nodded, but before she could answer, George had sprinted them both up the stairs.

SIXTEEN

George swung the ax deep into the log, filling the air with the sound of wood cracking in two. He'd already chopped and covered one wall of the garage with rows of winter kindling, but that hadn't done anything to quell his anger. June's words last night kept ringing in his head: *"Jack taught me."*

He hefted and swung the ax again, welcoming the burn in his shoulders and back. Willing it to deepen. If he could clear a forest he would. Anything to displace the pain in his heart. It burned him that another man was the person to reveal the ancient secret he'd been entrusted to keep from the woman he loved. A secret he'd wrestled with keeping for years.

How many times had he started then stopped himself from telling June, his daughter, and their granddaughter of their true heritage. Though, he'd left his brother little choice when he'd abandoned his wife. And in learning the truth from Jack, George had inadvertently been the catalyst for the bond between them.

"George, guests are going to be here soon," June called out from the back door, her voice stirring something primal inside of him. Lately, every time he was around her, it was like when they'd first met. He wanted to take her, claim her, make her his. More than that, he wanted to assure her with touch how sorry he was for leaving her. The pain he must have caused her with his stupid inability to control his wolf.

Sure, she'd forgiven him, but she didn't really know what she was doing, now did she? His brothers had tried to return his collar to him, but he'd fought it. The lure of the wolf was too sweet for him to turn away. He'd refused his family, and deep down he knew he no longer deserved them.

"Be right there!" He looked up from his stack of wood then took one last blast at a four-foot stump. A loud *crack* made him realize he'd used so much force the ax head snapped from the handle.

"Easy there," he told himself, dragging the dusty arm of his flannel across his wet brow. Thankfully, the tool had served today's purpose. He had enough wood already to last two winters. Intent on buying another later in the week, George tossed the handle, left the hunk of metal in the wood and headed to the house.

The kitchen was full of Thanksgiving aromas: turkey, sausage stuffing, garlic green bean casserole, and the best sweet potato pie he'd tasted in all his two-hundred-plus years of living. June always went all out for the holidays—but this being his first home in so long, she'd put in extra effort.

"Hey, Gramps," Zala said, as George entered the living room. She was sitting on the couch reading a book, the cubs curled in her lap. Next to her, sat Hank, glued to the Macy's Thanksgiving Day Parade being broadcast from the television. George doubted the man was truly interested, but, since his return, George could tell he made his son-in-law uncomfortable. The long absence and changed appearance were too much for the simple man to comprehend.

George had never understood what her daughter saw in Hank, but now he was glad she'd chosen such a basic fellow. Keeping their secret was that much easier when you were dealing with someone who didn't understand well enough to look closely at you. There was a possibility George was underestimating the man's intelligence, but one thing was for sure, he loved Aza, and there was no way he'd ever do anything to hurt her. The family secret was definitely safe.

"Good book?" George asked his granddaughter.

She smiled, and the glint in her eyes contained a bit of mischief. "It's a book about werewolves. I don't know why writers only ever think they can change with a full moon."

George laughed. "I'm not taking that on." And he didn't. Instead, he headed up the stairs to the shower.

Twenty minutes later, George was pulling a sweater over his head when he heard laughter down below. He came back downstairs in time to see June opening the door to Jack and Keith. The laughter had come from her. Jack was standing closest to her, smiling down, their shoulders almost touching.

George guessed he'd said something she found amusing. Largely amusing, judging from the volume of her laugh. It should have made him happy to see her smiling like that—instead, it made rage jolt up and out of his mouth in a low growl.

Still smiling, Jack made eye contact, his smile faltering some at what must have been an unpleasant expression in George's eyes. "Brother, I'd just asked about you. Had to make sure we weren't going to eat anything you'd hunted for us yourself tonight."

"If anyone looks like he's hunting, it's you, brother," George said, wrapping his arm around June's waist. His brothers had all been single for most of their lives, and he imagined that impacted their ability to comprehend the bond between a man and his wife.

Jack's eyebrows rose. "I'd never trespass."

"I hope you two aren't talking about me like I'm some piece of earth to be trod on and conquered," June said, eyeing them both.

Shamefaced, George looked down and followed June into the dining room where his daughter and granddaughter were bringing out serving plates.

"Uncle Jack! Uncle Keith!" Zala exclaimed as she set a dish of baked macaroni and cheese on the table before running to embrace them. "I'm so happy you came for the holidays," she said, her eyes glistening with tears.

George's heart clenched. He knew why this holiday was so joyous. It was the first one in four years that they'd all be spending together as a family. Thanks to him. The thought of the lost time again made his heart hurt.

If only....

June took him by the crook of the elbow and lifted a bottle of wine. "So, I'd say it's finally a good time for us to open this?" She was smiling now and he knew it was, in part, for his benefit. She'd always been good at reading his emotions. It wouldn't take a telepath to be able to sense that he was in low spirits now. And she was doing her best to bring them up. That made him sad too. She'd suffered on his account for four long years. Would there ever be a time when the woman wouldn't have to contort herself for his benefit?

"Don't recognize it?" she asked, holding the bottle closer.

George took the bottle of wine from June. Clearly old, from the faded lettering on the label, it took him a second. But suddenly he knew exactly where it'd come from. "Where'd you find this?"

"Downstairs."

George put it on the table and ran his hand over his jaw, trying not to frown.

Jack picked it up. "Is this what I think it is? A bottle from our old winery?"

"You guys had a winery?" Zala asked, curling one foot under her as she took her seat at the table. "How am I today-years-old and just learning this? What happened to it, Grandpa?"

"Ask your Uncle Jack. It was his winery."

Zala laughed.

"What's so funny?" Jack asked.

"It is funny. Go ahead, say it, I strike you as more the cultured sort than him," Keith said, thumbing in Jack's direction as he took his seat across from Zala.

"Well...it's probably better I leave that one alone," Zala said, smiling and folding her hands in front of her. "You gonna fill in the blanks, Uncle, or do I have to guess?"

"I was a farmer. I love the land, and I love wine. That the two loves should meet was only natural," Jack said.

The simple explanation shouldn't have bothered George, but it did. Life always seemed to work out nicely for his younger brother. He put his mind to a task and the next thing you knew, it was gold. George's eyes slid to June. She was laughing, along with his daughter and granddaughter, with Jack.

"I think that's very sweet, Uncle Jack. So, what happened to it?"

"Burned to the ground by the competition." Jack gave Zala a look and she turned to her mother, who just shook her head and passed a basket of hot butter rolls to her husband.

"Grace?" June said, clearly trying to put the conversation on a new track. The group responded by clasping hands and bowing their heads.

***

An hour later, June stood beside Aza at the sink when a rumble from the living room caused both of them to stop what they were doing and rush toward the noise.

"I saw the way you looked at her. I want you out of my house and don't ever come back," George growled.

"You spent too long in the wild, brother. You've forgotten how to think rationally," Jack spat back.

George's eyes were bright with anger, and he bared his canines. His wolf was seconds from making an appearance and ripping Jack to shreds. Keeping a wary eye on him, she said to Aza, "Take Hank upstairs, and don't come back until I call you."

Thankfully, Aza had been much more obedient since her father's return. She nodded once and they disappeared upstairs.

"You've thrown that in my face one too many times, little brother. It's time you learned to respect your Alpha." George punched Jack, and he flew through the window, knocking over a lamp and armchair in the process. By the time Jack landed, he'd taken his wolf form. George leapt after him, shifting as he sailed through the broken glass. The two squared off on the front lawn.

"Stop!" June said, deliberately standing between them in her fragile human form, praying George's fear of hurting her would keep him from ripping into Jack or her. "You're brothers!"

George's eyes swept from Jack to June to Zala, and his massive wolf shoulders slunk. The next instant, he'd dashed off into the woods. June let out a terrified gasp. He'd said himself that taking wolf form was something he shouldn't do yet. The lure was too potent. He hadn't been able to bring himself back the last time. What if she lost him for good this time? Yes, she knew she was strong enough to live without him, but if there was any way she could prevent that, she would.

She felt a hand on her arm, "Go, Mother! Find him and bring him back," Aza said.

Her gaze slid to Jack's. Those warm, brown eyes that had opened her mind to a whole new world held her with compassion and understanding. The pain of loving George had brought them closer together. And his steady presence since, had deepened their bond. Just looking at him gave her strength. He nodded to her, echoing Aza's words, "Go."

June stretched her arms and lifted her chin to the night sky. She inhaled as a woman and exhaled as her falcon. George in wolf was fast and cunning, but he was no match for June in flight.

A shadow dancing amongst shadows, George had covered many miles in minutes. June soared above, watching, admiring him as he raced and leapt over downed trees and small canyons. Happiness radiated from him in bright waves that she could see and feel even from her vantage point high above. George was free and more alive than he had been since he'd returned home to her. It was a beautiful thing.

June remembered the old saying, "If you love something, set it free." Perhaps it was time for her to set George free. Maybe their journey as mates had come to an end....

George ran for the better part of the night, until he reached the mountains of Kentucky. Early morning light crept over the mountain ridge, first a long silver thread outlining the horizon, then a yellow balloon floating in the sky.

June worried, not for herself, as falcons had little to fear from daylight, but for George. Wolves normally took shelter in daylight. If a human got sight of George the results could be deadly, more than likely for the human. And there was also the not so small issue of this enemy pack. They'd already found him once. But George continued to run, hurtling himself head-first into potential danger.

It was then that June realized what she must do. Landing on a boulder at the side of a great lake, she shifted into her own wolf form. She leapt down to the ground, more agile than any natural-born canine. The earth under her paws felt familiar and sweet, like an old friend welcoming her home. She loved the land as much as she loved the air but was grateful her magic made it such that she would never have to choose between the two. June ran, faster and faster, the love of speed in this new form mingling with her love of George, propelling her on even though the sun was now full in the sky, and danger was close.

June was so focused on George that she didn't see the trap until she fell head over heels into the ground. A series of deep barks burst from her throat, followed by one long howl before she instinctively transformed into her falcon, taking flight to avoid hitting the spiked ground beneath her. But before June cleared the top of the hole, a net came down, sealing her in. No matter how she struggled, the chained mail was too dense for her to penetrate. She was caught.

SEVENTEEN

A tightness in George's chest, like a great metal hand squeezing his heart, caused him to stop running abruptly. He knew the cause at once, feeling June's dismay before he heard her piercing howl.

His love had followed him, and now she was in grave danger. Taking in his surroundings for the first time, he realized he was deep in a thick, mountainous forest. Sunlight trickled through the dense canopy overhead. It wasn't a safe time to be out in wolf form. What if she'd been spotted by a hunter? Or worse, the others.

Dread filling his heart, George doubled back on his trail, stopping at the lake. He saw no sign of her. But she was close. He felt her, scented her, with everything he had. It wasn't until he saw the metal shield that he knew she'd fallen into a trap. At some point, he must have crossed into private property or a game reserve where hunters were still allowed to use pits to trap their prey.

Slowing his breath caused him to feel the emotions he'd been trying to keep at bay for the last several hours. Exquisite pain.

Guilt. Regret. How many times would he cause harm to this woman?

George howled, a long, deep anguished cry. June echoed his call. George lunged forward, his focus on getting to June. His paws landed briefly on the leaf-covered ground, and he heard a sound. A loud snap. The earth gave way beneath him. In his haste, he had failed to notice a second trap until he was falling deep into the hole.

One second his eyes glimpsed sky, in the next second his body had twisted, just in time to catch sight of a carpet made of foot-long metal spikes, all spearing up to greet him. With lightning speed, he extended his claws front and back, gripping the sides of the hole, not enough to stop him from falling, but enough to slow his momentum. When he reached the bottom of the hole and his stomach made contact with the spikes, it wasn't forceful enough to cause more than superficial damage.

Roaring, George kicked the spikes to their sides, breaking most of them in half. On principle, he hated the hunters who thought this an acceptable way to capture an animal. Suddenly he worried. Had June been harmed by spikes in her fall? The edge of the hole was too high for him to jump, especially without a running start. George dug his claws into the side of the hole, climbing toward the top. He was less than two feet from liberty when a metal tarp or blanket fell from the tree above, sealing him in total darkness.

Damn. Fucking hunters. His veins heated with rage as he thought about injured animals trapped and left to die in pits like this. George clawed at the walls of his cage, his coat dampened with sweat as his thoughts turned again to June.

I have failed her again....

EIGHTEEN

A soft chuckle broke the dark silence, and June soon realized it was bubbling up from her own chest. After everything she'd endured in recent weeks, to end up here, in the bottom of a pit? She couldn't help but laugh. Besides, the alternative—giving up—wouldn't help her to craft a solution.

Using her hands, she cleared a small circle around her, knocking over the closest of the hunter's sharp spikes with ease. Though they were deeply embedded in the earth, since learning of her magic, strength came more quickly each day.

Satisfied there was sufficient distance between her and the lethal spears, June stood to the full height of her human form, and she stared up. Her two eyelids became three as she tilted her entire head in the direction of the hole's cover. But even her falcon eyes weren't strong enough to pierce the darkness clinging to her skin like a lethal robe. She couldn't see her own hand in front of her and was grateful she'd glimpsed her surroundings, however quickly, as she'd descended into the pit. If her observations were correct, the metal sheet lay ten feet above her head. Surely, there was some way her magic would help her break free from this confinement. A woman who couldn't be held by another wolf's collar shouldn't be bound by mere mortals.

A nub of a thought surfaced, each tug producing more clarity. June had a toolbox. For years, she'd been using George's drill. It was about time she started using her own new-and-improved model.

She was aware of no reason her shifts had to be limited to animals she'd seen before. Or if there was, she wasn't aware. June closed her eyes, unnecessary in the dark, but old habits died hard. She raised her right arm, fist closed, and visualized it elongating, bone stretching skin, but not her own thin bone, one larger and stronger—elephantine. She felt as it grew, first inches and then feet, and though her magic made her strong, by the time her arm stretched three feet above her head her shoulder began to creak and groan.

Her own human joints weren't strong enough to sustain the added weight. She released the enormous mass at the end of her arm, returning her appendage to its natural state with a pained moan. There was a reason humans weren't born with giant hammers for hands.

Several minutes passed before June exhaled and opened her eyes. Rubbing her shoulder, she knew what she had to do. She closed her eyes again, and when she'd opened them, she was a Silverback gorilla in every way except for her left arm which was now six feet longer than the right.

Catapulting from one side of her walled cage to another, June quickly made it to the top, hammering her fist into the metal in one fell swoop.

Thwack.

As soon as her fist met the metal barrier, a booming noise resounded throughout the hole accompanied by a blinding blue light. Every muscle in June's body contracted, shrinking to a tenth of its original surface. A scream ripped from her throat as she writhed painfully, electric current snaking like lightning through her veins.

The metal covering was electrified with a high voltage.

The voltage was so high that June was unable to manage a shift into her falcon before hitting the ground with a thud that knocked the wind from her lungs. She lay there for a few minutes, dazed, as much by the blow as by the fact that she'd met her first limitation—she wasn't immune to electricity. But then again, why would she be? June curled into a fetal position on the side that hadn't struck the cover, though all of her body shuddered from pain. What a sick bunch of hunters, June thought as she lay there, gasping for breath, focusing her mind on calming the pain.

Once her heartbeat slowed, June lifted her head, looking up from between her arms. She gasped. Tears of joy stung her eyes. The night sky was visible in the hole's corner. The shield had moved, not enough to clear the hole's opening, at least not in her present form. A bee, however, didn't need nearly as much space.

Front legs wiping dust from hundreds of tiny hairs growing in her eyes was the first clue letting June know she'd shifted. Never before had she realized how many millions of hairs covered the small insects, but now that she was buzzing from the bottom to the top of the trap with the weight of a million dust particles clinging to each hair, she knew.

Virtually weightless now, June suddenly panicked at her own infinitesimal smallness. Everything felt so far away, yet there was something nearly claustrophobic about going from carrying a five-hundred-pound arm on a five-hundred-pound body to weighing less than a gram. Fortunately, her elevated tension increased her heartbeat and her distance from the base of the trap. In seconds, June realized she'd flown to the top of the hole.

The space between the edge of the trap's cover and the side of the hole was enough for dozens of workers to slip through. She had no problem gliding past in her honeybee form. To ensure she was out of reach of the hunters who'd laid the trap, June flew as high as she could and surveyed the area. Once she was sure no one was around, she shifted into her falcon, eyes scanning the land for George.

A howl alerted her to his presence on the other side of a small clearing. A gun metal blanket, covered with leaves lay on the ground between two pines. Had she not just climbed out of one herself, she would have easily missed it. Swooping down, June assumed, it too, was electrified.

In her present form, there was little she could do to combat powerful electrical currents without charring herself into a crisp. June hovered beside the hole. "George, it's me. I'm here for you."

"Thank God, you escaped."

"This shifting ability comes in handy. We'll get you out. Just give me a minute." June looked around the forest. In addition to stately pines, there were several mature birches, elms, maples, and a few saplings. She could think of no tool less conductive than wood.

Rising from the side of the trap, June shifted back into her silverback form, racing to a sapling nearby. At ten feet tall, it was the perfect length and width. June would easily be able to lever it under the edge of the metal lip, and while it was moist from recent rains, she might be able to pry open the hole before the electricity reached her.

But as she looked at the tree, a wave of sadness washed over her. Taking one life to save another didn't sit well with her. She remembered the birds coming to her aid the night she and George had their violent reunion. In her present state, she had a greater sensitivity to variant life forms than ever before. As she stood before the tree, she could feel its vitality, its will to live, and the comfort it took in being part of an arboreal community.

She thought back to all the wood she and George had stacked and burned over the years to heat their home and suddenly felt guilty. Good lord, was this incredible empathy the price to pay for her beautiful ability? June shook her head and held out her thick, leathery gorilla palms. The hunters who'd trapped her perceived her the same way she was looking at the tree. Who was she to cut that short just because it wasn't the same species as her? Not even for George. No, she couldn't. Not unless there was no other choice.

Nineteen

George cursed in frustration. Now that he was back in his human form, it was harder to hide from his emotions. Feelings of helplessness ate at his core. He was pissed, too, with himself for putting June in this situation. If only he hadn't let his jealousy get the better of him. A wolf was nothing if he couldn't control his emotions.

"George, I'm back. I'm going to get you out of there."

He laughed bitterly. "So, you're rescuing *me* now. Is that how it's going?"

"Welcome to a new dawn," June shot back.

George stood, naked and ashamed, at the bottom of the pit as the metal cover slid back, then flipped to its side. "Is that what I think it is?"

June, in a silverback version of herself, stood at the top, holding a small tree. "You're lucky. It was already lying on the ground. Probably knocked down in the last storm."

George inhaled. He wasn't sure what she meant when she said he was lucky, but he knew what he thought. The woman was miraculous, her abilities astonishing.

She guided the tree into the hole. When it touched bottom, George gripped the trunk and shimmied to the top.

"I don't know what to say first, thank you or I'm sorry," he said, watching mesmerized as June shifted effortlessly into her young human form.

"If you want to make me truly happy, tell me you'll stop running when things get uncomfortable."

George took her hand, soft and warm, in his and pressed his lips to her skin. He felt her whole body quiver from that one touch. After all these years, they still had that effect on each other. He wanted to take her right there on the forest floor, but first, he had something to do. George reached up and fingered the gold pendant at his neck. "I'll do you one better." He ripped the collar from his body, lobbing it deep into the lake's dark waters.

June gasped. "George, what have you done?"

George's eyes fell to his bare feet. "I can't have you and my wolf. And you are more important to me. I never want to lose you again."

"But George—"

He didn't need to hear the words to know what she was going to say. He didn't want to hear them. He didn't want to talk. He turned to her, slid one arm around her waist and pulled her to him. He felt her naked breasts, silky and warm against the skin of his chest. Using his index finger, he lifted her chin. She wasn't talking, but the fiery gaze in her eyes spoke volumes: deep, abiding love, mixed with worry and hungry yearning.

Unable to refuse his own desire, he pressed his lips against hers. A flood of passion enveloped them both, and, for a moment, they were able to forget about everything but their own all-consuming physical needs.

TWENTY

The days between Thanksgiving and the week before Christmas normally flew by, but after learning about her unique lineage, they rushed at lightning speed. June had the strange feeling that danger stalked her family. Several times, she thought she saw things out of the corner of her eye, but when she turned to face them head on, nothing was there. She chalked it up to all of the changes she'd been through in the last few months. Learning the truth about herself had been a lot.

George hadn't been in the best of moods either. Oh, he tried to put up a good face, but June knew the man, better than she knew herself in many respects. His wolf had been a part of him for more than two-hundred years. As difficult as it was for her to make room for a new identity, his struggles were far more challenging. He'd amputated a part of himself for her and he was now moving through the world like a man who was missing an integral piece of himself.

June was grateful when a heavy snow began to fall Thursday night. It didn't stop until early Sunday morning. When it did, the drifts were as high as the hood of a car in several places, which gave George purpose.

He busied himself digging out first their driveway with a shovel and once he was able to get the truck out, he drove to several of the neighbors' homes to help them dig out. Each night he returned home exhausted. June drew him a hot bath. He'd soak, come down, nibble at dinner, and then make an excuse to go to bed early. When she joined him later, they made love. It was warm and tender and June knew that when George took her body, he was feeling her wolf as much as he felt her. Being close to it helped him, released him from some of his suffering, but no matter how much they made love, nothing she could give him would ever be a substitute for what he'd lost. George was in mourning, and his grief would persist for the rest of his life.

Christmas morning arrived with fresh snowfall. June awoke to an empty bed, sitting up and stretching, a smile curved her lips. She threw the covers back and padded downstairs to the living room where warm air from the fireplace greeted her. The scent of fresh coffee and vanilla wafted through the ground floor.

"Mmmm, that smells delicious. What is it?"

Smiling, George turned around with a plate extended. On it was a thick slice of French toast, covered in syrup, strawberries and whipped cream. "Your favorite."

June steepled her index finger in front of her lips. After all of these years, he still surprised her with her favorite dishes and she loved him for it. "This is how you start Christmas morning," she said, taking the plate from his hands and stretching up on her tiptoes to plant a warm kiss on his lips.

She took her seat at the table and George took his seat opposite. "I was hoping you'd give me some taste test feedback before everyone arrived."

"I'm happy to oblige. There are a few things I want to do before they get here, too."

"Really? What does my beautiful bride have in mind?"

"You'll see. Christmas is supposed to be a time of surprises."

Thirty minutes later, after June had approved the recipe and they'd cleared the dishes, she took George by the hand. She stopped at the tree and lifted a small gold box from beneath it. When she handed it to George, his right eyebrow rose. "Normally, we wait for everyone."

"An exception every now and then can be a good thing. Go on, open it."

George hesitated, and June nodded again. Finally, he shrugged and tugged at the wrapping paper covering the end of the small box. Coming apart easily, he let the paper fall to the floor. All that was left in his hand was a small black box. George narrowed his eyes. "What have you done?"

June tilted her head. "Open the lid and find out."

George lifted the lid and his mouth dropped. He shook his head. "How on earth did you find this?"

June reached in and lifted George's amulet from the small box. "A woman has her ways."

He stepped back as though burned by fire. "June, I don't know how you found this, but you shouldn't have brought it back into the house. I'm never going to use it again. I can't."

June had spent a full day as a carp scouring the lake's floor, dodging the dangling hooks of dozens of ice fishermen. There was no way she was taking no for an answer. Mostly because her one day in fish form was nothing in comparison to the agony George would suffer if he cut his wolf out of his life entirely.

"George, your shifts aren't the problem. If you think about all the times you've shifted and lost yourself, there's been one constant." June paused to give him time to recall, placing her hand on his. She could feel his large muscles tense and strong. She met his strength with her own steely-eyed gaze. "We were apart."

George's lips parted in protest. June cupped his jaw with her palm and looked up into his eyes tenderly, "You said it yourself, seventy years ago—we are made for each other. This protection is a two-way street."

George sighed.

"From now on, we run together," June said.

George covered her hand and kissed the palm, sending heat rippling up her arm. "You know how badly I want this, but, as much as I do, I can't take it." He held the box out to June. "I just don't trust myself."

"Trust *me*." She shook her head and stepped even closer to him. She could see the battle waging inside of him. He was a man dangling from a mountainside, clinging to a fraying rope with one hand, being offered a ladder that descended into clouds and who knew what else. For hundreds of years he'd been the mountain for himself, for his brothers, for his wife, for their daughter and granddaughter. To allow someone else to be all of that for him was a leap of faith he didn't have the wings for. June stepped up on her tiptoes and kissed the man she'd loved so fiercely for seven decades. "Trust *us*. Together we are everything we need."

George leaned his forehead down until it rested against hers. "I married a helluva woman, didn't I?"

"And don't you ever forget it." June reached up around George's neck, clasping the necklace in one swift movement. "Merry Christmas, my love."

"Your love is the best gift a man ever could have hoped for."

"And it's all yours. Forever."

EPILOGUE

The snow muffled all sound but the beating of June's heart as she ran from the treeline of the Enchanted Forest into the sprawling fields surrounding her house. Above her, Orion's Belt shone luminous, and beside her, George stretched his front legs into a galloping sprint as they both raced to catch up with Zala and the quickly growing pups.

As June had expected, their granddaughter mastered her first shift shortly after George sat them all down to explain the family legacy. Probably due to her open mind, all Zala needed to access her abilities was knowledge of their existence.

Since discovering her truth, the five of them ran together regularly, as much to teach Zala as to enjoy the exhilaration that came from racing through the world in their animal forms. Zala grew stronger every day, and both June and George sensed her powers were great—greater even than June's.

Aza's change hadn't happened yet, but June was relatively certain her daughter's day would come. She just needed the right catalyst. If her own life had taught her anything, it was that no matter how old you were; it was never too late to discover new things about yourself.

Life was full of surprises, many of them beautiful. She'd been writing again. And she had another secret to reveal this evening.

As Zala ran ahead toward the house with the pups, June slowed. George reduced his speed as well. "Is everything okay?"

"I have a surprise for you," June whispered once her granddaughter was so far away there was no chance her wolf ears would pick up the words.

George looked at June, his eyes, one blue and one green, sparkling. "Am I meant to guess?"

June laughed. "I doubt you would guess this in a thousand years. I know that I never would have."

"You've found a way to shift into a fire-breathing dragon?"

June cocked her head, taking in the stars out of the corner of her eyes. "That's an idea worth considering, but no. I haven't done any dragon-shifting just yet." June shifted back into human form, and George lurched back then forward, his nose in the air, sniffing obsessively.

"June! You aren't?"

June covered her face with her hands as George shifted into human form and wrapped his arms around her, burying his nose into her neck. "Yes, I am. Call the Guinness Book of World Records, if such a thing still exists. If it doesn't, resurrect it and let them know that the first ninety-two-year-old pregnant woman lives and breathes!"

George stepped back and looked at her. "You truly are a marvel."

"Life is the marvel, and I see we're just scratching the surface."

"Come on, let's go home." Her heart stuttered at the sound of the word on his lips. After all this time, the old farmhouse did feel like a home again. He smiled at her, as if sensing her thoughts. "We've got some news to share."

June shifted and George followed, both eager to share the news that they were expanding their Dargin pack. Halfway to the house, a scream, sharp as a blade, pierced the air.

Zala.

"Go." George's voice, laced with urgency and fear, shot through her head. "I'm right behind you."

June shifted into her falcon, heart racing as she shook the air with her powerful wings. But in that blood-chilling moment, she didn't need the advantage of height or keen eyesight to understand the gravity of their situation. The family she had fought so hard to reunite was in danger once again. The others had found them...

THE END

***

Thank you for reading June & George's story. I'd love to keep in touch! Sign up for my newsletter to learn about new releases, deleted scenes, author shenanigans, and so much more! www.tanajenkins.com

ALSO BY TANA

Sica the Assassin is the ultimate prize in the master's twisted game, an alien experiment of extraordinary power in a realm where the dichotomy between science and sorcery has shattered. Sica's strength lies in his ability to shape reality itself, but when an interrogation goes wrong, the boundaries between reality and nightmare begin to blur.

To complete his mission, Sica must form a shaky alliance with Dahlia, a cursed witch, bound to hunt his kind. Trust is a precious commodity, and with the stakes high and danger everywhere, each decision could mean the difference between life and death.

The biggest obstacle of all, however, may be the intense attraction growing between Sica and Dahlia. Engineered assassins aren't meant to feel, let alone fall in love with the enemy.

With the fabric of his reality in flux, Sica must face the ultimate question: who is really in control? With twists and turns at every step, and a heart-stopping tale of forbidden love set amidst intergalactic intrigue, Sica's story challenges everything you thought you knew about the nature of truth and the limits of desire.

Acknowledgements

First and foremost, thank you to the love of my life, Mr. Jenkins. You've always been my rock, and the best parts of every hero are shaped by your influence.

That said, this book wouldn't have been possible without the assistance of several amazing romance authors. DK Marie, Maggie Eliot, Sky Voss, Cana Owens, and Natalie Dunbar, I can't thank you enough. Your thought-provoking critiques have consistently pushed me to improve, and your feedback was invaluable in shaping this story.

I'm also deeply thankful to Uncle John for taking time away from watching the Lions' first winning streak, in order to discuss a wolf prowling through the night. And, thank you Melanie Giovannone for stopping everything to help with line edits. You're an awesome friend and writer! Big thanks to The Get Write To It Girls, K.T. Bond and Linda for keeping me accountable by showing up in our writing groups week after week. It truly takes a village, and I'm so glad we're in each other's. As always, thank you to Mama Lauree and Mama Susan for years of love, support and encouragement.

But most importantly, my enduring appreciation goes to my remarkable readers. Your time and support mean the world to me, and I am so grateful for every single one of you. You make every second of this journey worthwhile, and I am profoundly honored that you choose to get lost in my stories. From the bottom of my heart, thank you!

ABOUT THE AUTHOR

Named 2022 Debut Author of the Year by RSJ, former attorney Tana Jenkins is a Pushcart Nominee, On the Farside ParanormalFinalist, and EMMA Award-Winner for Clean & Sweet Romance, who has always been passionate about the magic of love. Her sweet and paranormal romances bring this magic to life using richly imagined plots featuring diverse women who are typically as lovable as they are quirky. And as a nod to the notion that love knows no bounds, her romances, which have hit Barnes & Noble and Amazon bestseller lists, are almost always interracial.

After practicing law in several locales, including on the beautiful island of St. Croix, she writes from the Great Lakes region, which features in her sweet, beach romances. There, she lives her own HEA with her college sweetheart and their adorable rescue, Albee. When not penning the next novel or planning beach escapades, she can be found snuggled up with a good book and a bowl of ice cream.

Don't miss out on exclusive bonus scenes, sneak peeks, cover reveals, and more by signing up for her newsletter at www.tanajenkins.com.

Printed in Great Britain
by Amazon